SURVIVAL TAILS

ENDURANCE IN ANTARCTICA

Book 2

By Katrina Charman

LITTLE, BROWN AND COMPANY
NEW YORK BOSTON

Copyright © 2018 by Katrina Charman
Illustrations copyright © 2018 by Owen Richardson

Cover art copyright © 2018 by Owen Richardson. Cover design by Nicole Brown. Cover copyright © 2018 by Hachette Book Group, Inc.

Little, Brown and Company
Hachette Book Group
1290 Avenue of the Americas, New York, NY 10104
Visit us at LBYR.com

First Edition: December 2018

Little, Brown and Company is a division of Hachette Book Group, Inc. The Little, Brown name and logo are trademarks of Hachette Book Group, Inc.

The publisher is not responsible for websites (or their content) that are not owned by the publisher.

Library of Congress Cataloging-in-Publication Data
Names: Charman, Katrina, author.
Title: Endurance in Antarctica / by Katrina Charman.
Description: First edition. | New York ; Boston : Little, Brown and Company, 2018. | Series: Survival tails ; book 2 | Summary: "A group of sled dogs must race to survive during a perilous journey across Antarctica"— Provided by publisher.
Identifiers: LCCN 2017059759| ISBN 9780316477895 (hardcover) | ISBN 9780316477901 (trade pbk.) | ISBN 9780316477888 (ebook) | ISBN 9780316477871 (library ebook edition)
Subjects: LCSH: Shackleton, Ernest Henry, Sir, 1874–1922—Juvenile fiction. | CYAC: Shackleton, Ernest Henry, Sir, 1874–1922—Fiction. | Imperial Trans-Antarctic Expedition (1914–1917)—Fiction. | Sled dogs—Fiction. | Dogs—Fiction. | Survival—Fiction. | Endurance (Ship)—Fiction. | Antarctica—Discovery and exploration—Fiction.
Classification: LCC PZ7.1.C495 End 2018 | DDC [Fic]—dc23
LC record available at https://lccn.loc.gov/2017059759

ISBNs: 978-0-316-47789-5 (hardcover), 978-0-316-47790-1 (pbk.), 978-0-316-47788-8 (ebook)

Printed in the United States of America

LSC-H

10 9 8 7 6 5 4 3 2 1

For Maddie, Piper, and Riley

CHAPTER 1
SAMSON

July 1914

Samson panted, trying to stay cool as he kept pace with the dogs at the front of the pack. Each dog was determined to stay one step ahead of the others, trying to prove himself. Like him, they were mutts—a mixture of more than one breed: Newfoundland, Saint Bernard, wolfhound—specifically selected for their size, strength, and thick fur.

Samson imagined he was running free in the Antarctic, a cool breeze blasting against his face as he bounded through deep, unblemished snow never before trodden on by human or dog. He chased his companions across ice-covered lakes until his legs and lungs burned. He breathed in air so fresh and pure that he felt he could run forever.

One of the dogs beside him edged ahead, grinning as he began to overtake Samson. Samson grinned back, accepting the challenge and digging down even further inside himself to go faster, faster! He quickly caught up with the other dog so that there was barely a nose between them. Samson pulled farther ahead, watching the dog's expression as he took the lead. But instead of racing faster, the dog suddenly pulled back as though afraid to continue.

Samson turned to run for victory just in time to see the brick wall enclosing the dogs' exercise yard looming dead ahead. He skidded to a halt, narrowly avoiding a collision as his attention slammed back to reality.

A whistle sounded, and he and the nine other dogs in his group were led back into the building that housed their kennels. Samson reluctantly followed, his daydream fading as each dog was put into their own cage. Each dog's name was written in chalk on a board hung above. The kennels were dark and the atmosphere hot and stifling. Samson's thick fur was much better suited to the freezing temperatures of his Canadian homeland than the smoggy, humid London air.

Like Samson, the other dogs were restless. With almost a hundred dogs in such close proximity, a brawl broke out practically every time a group was let out for daily exercise. Today was no different. Exercise time was always too short, and Samson's muscles were still tightly knotted from being imprisoned in his kennel all night. The other dogs hated being locked back up. They growled warnings to their kennel neighbors in frustration, snapping their jaws and baring their teeth, each attempting to assert authority over the other. Those dogs would never be chosen for the expedition, Samson thought with a shake of his head. They were too wild.

He tried to settle in a comfortable position in what little space he had, resting his chin on his paws, hoping for a little nap despite the constant yapping and bickering. As he dozed, his mind wandered, filled with thoughts of what might lie ahead. He couldn't wait for the expedition to begin. To be on a ship heading off toward adventure.

The famous explorer Ernest Shackleton had requested that ninety-nine dogs be brought over from their homeland to accompany him on his next journey into the unknown. Shackleton planned to be the first person to make the trip across land from one side of Antarctica to the other, while the Ross sea party set up supply depots on the opposite side. Shackleton would be looking for dogs who were strong, able to lead, not quick to brawl. Samson knew he could be all those things, but more than that, he wanted to discover new frontiers and make his mark on the world just as Shackleton had.

A snuffle came from his left, and Samson opened one eye to peer through the wire cage at the dog next to him. Samson's neighbor was smaller than most of the other dogs, and his fur wasn't as full. Where Samson had long white-and-gray fur that hung in his eyes, this dog's fur was brown, short, and wiry. Samson remembered him from the voyage over from Canada. The dog had been sick most of the journey. While the other dogs had relished the spray in their faces from the crashing waves, and the salty tang of the ocean air, this dog had barely left his kennel. Samson wondered how he had been chosen to come in the first place. If he couldn't handle a simple boat trip, the poor fellow wouldn't survive the journey to Antarctica, let alone the expedition.

The dog snuffled again.

"Is everything all right?" Samson whispered, so the other dogs wouldn't hear. They had mostly ignored the dog when he was keeping to himself in his kennel, and Samson had been too caught up in his own excitement about the journey ahead. But if they sensed a crying dog in their midst, he'd have no chance.

The dog glanced over at Samson, then dropped his head to his paws again with a groan.

"I don't belong here." The dog sighed. "Look at these other dogs." He glanced up again. "Look at you! I can barely keep up with them out in the yard, let alone haul a great hulking sled behind me."

Samson moved closer to the wire cage dividing them. "I'm sure you're not all that bad," he said. "Besides, we'll be trained first. There will be plenty of time to build up your strength and stamina."

The dog sniffed. "You think so?"

Samson nodded. "I'm sure of it. The humans must have seen something in you to have picked you to come to England in the first place. C'mon, what are you best at?"

The dog hesitated. "Well...I'm a good hunter," he said.

"There you go," Samson replied. "Don't give up just yet."

The dog's eyes brightened. "I'm Bummer," he said with a shy smile.

Samson smiled back. "Samson. Nice to meet you."

Bummer was quiet for a moment and Samson lay back down.

"What do you suppose will happen to us if we're not chosen?" Bummer asked.

Samson paused. He wasn't sure of the answer, and he wasn't all that certain that Bummer *would* be chosen, but he didn't want to dampen the smaller dog's spirits now that he'd started to cheer up. "Probably be sent back to Canada," he said. "But that won't happen to us. Think positively. I'm strong and fast, and you're a good hunter. That'll be worth something."

Before Bummer could reply, the dog in the cage on his other side began laughing. "Don't lie to him," he howled. "The runt has no chance and you know it."

Samson growled, but the dog ignored him, leaning so close against the cage that it looked as if dog and wire were merging into one. "You're too small, too slow, too weak," he told Bummer.

Samson growled another warning at the dog as Bummer backed into the corner of his cage, his tail between his legs.

"See?" The dog laughed. "He hasn't got an ounce of courage. The main thing you need in the wilderness is courage. Expeditions are not for the fainthearted. He doesn't belong here with the likes of us."

Bummer whimpered.

"That's enough!" Samson barked, jumping up against his cage. The other dog did the same as Bummer cowered in the middle.

"What's all this noise about, Amundsen?" a man asked, hurrying in from the yard. He glanced at the two dogs growling at each other and opened Amundsen's cage. "Time for some exercise," the man said. "Looks like you could burn off a bit of energy."

Another human joined the first and they opened some of the other cages, leashing five dogs each to lead them outside to the paved yard.

"I'm glad we're not in Amundsen's exercise group," Samson muttered as he watched them leave. Amundsen was clearly bad news. Samson was sure he and Bummer hadn't heard the last of him.

"Did you see Shackleton's advertisement?" a third man asked a fourth a few cages down as he swept Amundsen's cage. Samson's ears pricked up. The man pulled a piece of paper out of his pocket and unfolded it. "I was thinking of applying," he said, passing it over to his companion.

" 'Men wanted for hazardous journey,' " the other man read out loud. " 'Small wages. Bitter cold. Long months of complete darkness. Constant danger. Safe return doubtful. Honor and recognition in case of success.' "

He folded up the paper and handed it back. "You're a braver man than me," he said. "I wouldn't last five minutes in those conditions. It's bad enough working these kennels in the winter."

Samson turned to Bummer. "Did you hear that?" he asked, his tail wagging as the men moved away to clean out the other vacant cages. *"Honor and recognition!"*

Bummer shook his head. "All I heard was *constant danger*. Amundsen was right. I don't belong here."

"Don't listen to Amundsen. He's just trying to spook as many dogs as he can so that he'll have a better chance of getting in. Look at him," Samson said, nodding toward the yard, where Amundsen seemed to be holding court, with six dogs surrounding him and listening intently to his every word. "He's a bully. Plain and simple. Shackleton won't want dogs like that on the trip."

Amundsen's ears pricked up. He shot a glance over at Samson, baring his teeth in a grin.

Bummer looked at Samson uncertainly.

"Just wait and see," Samson reassured him. "Soon you and I will be off on a grand adventure, and Amundsen will be far, far behind us."

CHAPTER 2
BUMMER

July 1914

Bummer couldn't get the words *constant danger* out of his mind. It was all he could think about when awake, all he dreamed about when he got what little sleep he could. Worst of all, he couldn't stop thinking about what would happen to him when he *wasn't* chosen—when neither his master back home nor Shackleton wanted him.

"He's here!" Samson barked. "Shackleton is here." His tail wagged so hard that it *smack, smack, smack*ed against the wire cage as fast as Bummer's heartbeat.

"What do you think we'll have to do?" Bummer asked, pressing his face against the wire to get a glimpse of the man who held their future in his hands.

Samson frowned, then his eyes brightened. "Maybe a bit of running?" he suggested. "I hope it's running. I'm good at running."

"I bet you're good at everything," Bummer said under his breath.

Samson was one of the biggest dogs, if not *the* biggest dog there. Even though his fur was thick and full, Bummer could still see the curve of his muscles and the power they held. Samson was likely to be chosen as soon as Shackleton laid eyes on him, and Amundsen along with him.

It suddenly occurred to Bummer that being between two of the largest, strongest dogs was not likely to put him in the best light.

A row of men lined up, each taking a dog from the kennel to lead them out into the yard. Bummer took a deep breath as Samson gave him a reassuring nod. The dogs stood in a long row with their allocated humans, their backs against the wall as Shackleton stood before them, notebook and pencil in hand. He was not a tall man, Bummer thought, but he had the presence of a giant. In his smart gray pinstripe suit and black shoes so highly polished that the morning light glinted off them, there was no doubt that he was the alpha. He paraded slowly up and down, pausing every so often to examine a dog or scribble something in his pad.

He shook his head at two of the men and they took their dogs away, leading them out through the tall wooden gates at the opposite end of the yard.

"Where are they going?" Bummer whispered to Samson.

"Isn't it obvious?" Amundsen snapped before Samson could answer. "They're no good."

Bummer lowered his head and tried to swallow down the huge lump in his throat as the dogs were led past, their eyes wide with confusion and a fear that matched his own. They were bigger than he was and likely stronger. If they weren't chosen, Bummer thought, he had no chance.

"Swap places with me," Bummer said, trying to squeeze past Samson to move farther down the line, closer to some slightly smaller dogs where he wouldn't be so dwarfed, but the man holding his leash pulled him back firmly.

"Stay calm," Samson whispered out of the corner of his mouth. "Just do what I do."

Bummer gave a quick nod and straightened up, trying to keep his legs from shaking as he mirrored Samson's stance. Stand firm. Tail straight. Head high.

He tried to focus as Shackleton neared. Resisting the urge to watch what was happening, he stared straight ahead. Finally, a dark shadow fell over Bummer and he held his breath, not daring to look Shackleton in the eye.

"These two," Shackleton said.

Samson looked at Bummer with a wide grin. Bummer stared back. He couldn't believe it! He'd been chosen. He moved to follow Samson as he was led back to the kennels, but his leash held firm.

Amundsen gave a harsh laugh beside him. "You didn't think he meant *you*?" he said, following Samson.

Bummer felt his heart drop out of his chest. What had he expected? He wondered why he'd ever hoped he might have a chance. His brother had told him as much before Bummer had left Canada. He was the one who was supposed to come to London, not Bummer. It was only because their master had changed his mind at the last minute—hadn't wanted to give up his *best dog*—that Bummer had been offered up in his place.

He hadn't belonged there and he didn't belong here, either.

Bummer's tail sagged as he watched the lucky dogs who had been chosen being led to the kennels, their tails wagging and heads held high in triumph, while those who hadn't made the cut were led out of the gate. Bummer could feel their disappointment growing in his own belly as he waited to be led the same way.

A set of bricks was laid out across the yard in a wavy path. The remaining dogs were given a new task—to weave in and out of the bricks as fast as they could. It seemed easy enough, Bummer thought, but it had rained earlier that morning and the cobblestones were slick with water.

A sudden determination came over him as he was led to the starting point. Shackleton hadn't cut him yet. He still had a chance to prove himself. Bummer dug his claws into the ground and ducked his head low, trying to ignore the roar of blood in his ears and the tremor in his legs.

"You're still here," he whispered to himself. "Don't give up yet. You're still here."

Shackleton held up his shiny golden pocket watch and shouted, "Go!"

Bummer ran as fast and hard as he could, swiftly

weaving in and out between the bricks as though he'd done it a thousand times before. He was almost at the end when something small and gray darted ahead, making him lose focus.

A mouse.

Bummer's front paw slipped and he flew forward, tripping over the last brick, tumbling head over paw to land in a heap at the wall.

Shackleton shook his head, making a mark on his notepad.

Bummer glanced around desperately as his man came over with his leash. He didn't want to leave! Not when he'd finally found a friend, not when he'd had just the tiniest bit of hope that he might actually be chosen.

He spotted the mouse again, zipping along the bottom edge of the wall toward Shackleton. Bummer pulled away as the man leaned down to leash him, and raced toward Shackleton at full pelt, skidding right between his legs to dive at the blur. Then he turned back, lifting his prize in the air between his jaws triumphantly.

The tiny mouse he'd caught wriggled and squealed, shaking a paw at Bummer. "Let me go, you overgrown rat!"

Shackleton stared at Bummer and the mouse for a moment before whispering something to the man with the leash. The man nodded and headed toward Bummer, eyeing him warily.

Bummer's head drooped. What had he been thinking? He'd tried to make one last attempt at showing Shackleton what he could do but had only ended up looking like a wild animal. He gently lowered the mouse to the ground, letting him go. "Sorry," he said.

The mouse gave a shrill "Hmmph!" and scampered off.

Bummer sat down to allow the man to leash him, then started toward the gate, but the man pulled firmly in the other direction.

"Back to the kennels, you daft dog!" the man huffed. "Are you sure you want this one?" he called over to Shackleton.

Shackleton gave Bummer a small smile, then nodded. "I like his spirit."

Bummer strutted back to the kennels, feeling bigger than Amundsen and Samson combined.

CHAPTER 3

BUMMER

August 1914

It had been a tense few weeks while they'd waited at the kennels to be brought to Plymouth, where Shackleton's ship, the *Endurance*, was docked. As much as he hated sailing, Bummer had to admit that the ship was impressive. It had been specially adapted to withstand the harsh conditions of the Antarctic, with a thick frame and hull reinforced at every possible point. Its bow was sleek and narrow, resembling the sharp-edged blade of an ax, able to cut through thick pack ice as easily as water. Three tall masts reached to the sky and a shorter funnel stood at the stern of the ship, and four sturdy lifeboats—two on each side—hung out over the water from the top deck.

The sixty-nine dogs chosen to join Shackleton's Imperial Trans-Antarctic Expedition had their own open-fronted wooden kennels, which ran the length of both sides of the top deck. To his relief, Bummer and Samson had remained kennel neighbors at the bow, the front end of the ship. The dogs were kept chained to their kennels, but the chains were long and loose and the dogs were often released as long as they didn't cause any trouble or get in the crew's way. Bummer preferred to stay in the relative safety of his kennel, as far away from Amundsen as it was possible to get on a ship surrounded by water.

"I knew he'd be chosen," Bummer whispered to Samson, nodding down the deck at Amundsen.

"Well, I *was* right about one thing," Samson said with a grin.

"What's that?"

"That you and I would both be chosen," Samson said.

Bummer shook his head in disbelief. There were so many other dogs who would have been far better suited to the expedition than him. He still couldn't quite believe it. He watched the humans on the quayside, waving farewell, and couldn't help but wonder how long it would be until they returned to civilization.

"Where's the boss?" one of the men called out, scanning the deck for Shackleton as he hurried past. "Britain has declared war against Germany!"

The men called Shackleton the boss, and the dogs had taken to doing the same.

"What does that mean?" Samson asked. "Are we still going to Antarctica?"

"Not if the humans need this ship for their war," Bummer replied, feeling an odd mixture of disappointment and relief all at once.

Samson looked distraught. "But I wanted to make my mark on the world. I want to be known for doing something...amazing." He sighed.

Bummer couldn't help but feel disappointed for his friend, even if he wasn't sure he felt the same way. The excitement of being chosen for the expedition had quickly worn off and slowly turned into a nauseating dread in the pit of his stomach that he wasn't entirely sure was due to seasickness.

"I'm sure there will be other expeditions," Bummer said to himself as much as to Samson.

They strained against their chains as Shackleton appeared on deck, waving a piece of paper in his hand.

He gathered the men around. "It's a telegram from the Admiralty," he told them. Men and dogs moved closer, eager to hear the news. "Britain is at war with Germany," he said solemnly. "But we have been sent word that we can continue with the expedition." He held up the telegram for all to see. "It says: *Proceed*!"

The men cheered and the dogs barked. Samson howled in delight that he would get his big adventure after all. To his surprise, despite the fear of the unknown, Bummer couldn't help but feel a burst of excitement, too. This was his chance, he thought, to prove that he did belong. After a long pause, Bummer added his barks and howls to the chorus.

"Are you not pleased?" a voice purred from above. "You don't seem as excited as the others."

Bummer peered up to see a cat with patches of brown and black and white fur lounging on his kennel roof, her tail waving hypnotically back and forth.

"Of course, just a little nervous about what lies ahead, that's all. What are you doing on board?" he asked.

"I came with my human, the carpenter," she said. "I'm Mrs. Chippy."

"Aren't you afraid of being the only cat on a ship full of dogs?" Bummer asked.

"Should I be?" Mrs. Chippy asked with a sly smile.

"Not of me, I suppose." Bummer gestured down the deck toward Amundsen. "But maybe some of the others."

"Don't worry about me," Mrs. Chippy said, standing to stretch out her back. "I'm not so easily scared."

"Have you been on a ship before?" Bummer asked.

Mrs. Chippy shook her head. "No, but I'm sure it's no different from being on land," she said. "Better, in fact... On land you don't have food readily available at any time of day or night. Just look at all that fresh fish." She peered over the edge of the ship, licking her jaws.

Bummer laughed. "Not so easy to catch, though."

Mrs. Chippy frowned. "I'll find a way," she said. "Or I'll pester my human until he catches some for me."

She slunk off along the kennel roofs, ignoring the barking as she passed. If Bummer hadn't known better, he'd have thought she was goading them on purpose. He lay in his kennel, listening to the ongoing revelry.

"Bummer!" Samson called out as the crew let the

dogs off their chains. "Come and meet Sally and the others."

Bummer padded over to where Samson was chatting excitedly with a group of dogs about their journey ahead.

"This is Bummer," Samson told the group. "He's a smart one, so you'll want him on your sled team."

A couple of the dogs studied Bummer doubtfully, but before they could say anything, a dog stepped forward. She was larger than Bummer—but then so were most of the dogs—and had thick, silky, light gray fur that shone in the sunlight. Her deep blue eyes sparkled as she smiled at him warmly. "Nice to meet you, Bummer," she said. "I'm Sally."

Bummer returned her smile gratefully. "I'm not sure I'll be on any sled team," he muttered. "I'm still not sure I should be here at all."

"Nonsense," Sally said. "I had to leave my mate back home, but I know we were all chosen for a reason. I'm sure you'll discover your place soon enough."

"His place is at the back of the ship with the pigs," Amundsen snarled, pushing the other dogs aside. He was flanked by two of the fiercest-looking dogs Bummer had ever seen. One of them—Hercules—had thick fur as black as night, with eyes to match. The other had an elongated jaw and teeth so sharp he looked more wolf than dog, which was how, Bummer supposed, he got the name Wolf.

"You want to know why you were chosen?" Amundsen asked. "It's so that if the humans run out of food they'll have more fresh meat on board." Amundsen roared with laughter, and a few of the other dogs laughed along uneasily. Bummer tried as hard he could not to show the fear in his eyes.

"Bummer's a better dog than you," Samson growled, moving to stand beside Bummer.

"Bummer?" Amundsen laughed more loudly. "Is that what they called you?"

Sally stood on Bummer's other side and he suddenly felt a little braver, and a little surer of himself.

"I'm as good as any dog here," Bummer said, his heart hammering against his ribs. "I was chosen by the boss just like the rest of you."

Amundsen leaned forward, so close that Bummer could feel his hot, sour breath on his face. "Your friends aren't always going to be around to protect you," he whispered. "What will you do when you find yourself all alone out in the wilderness?"

Sally snarled, but Amundsen ignored her. He strutted back to his kennel with Wolf and Hercules on either side.

"Are you all right?" Sally asked.

Bummer nodded, his heart pounding with a mixture of fear and amazement that he'd stood up for himself—although he doubted that he would have been as brave if Samson and Sally hadn't been by his side. A brown blur ran past, flying across the kennel roofs as the deck rumbled and shook with the weight of sixty oversized dogs chasing after it.

"Mrs. Chippy!" Bummer yelled, taking off after the other dogs. He jumped, trying to see over the heads of the ever-increasing number of dogs surrounding the cat. All he could see was fur and jaws and tails, and Amundsen leading the pack as they closed in on the terrified cat.

She hissed at Amundsen as he drew nearer, striking out at his face with extended claws. Amundsen let out a roar of rage and reared back as Mrs. Chippy frantically lashed out again and again, trying to keep him and the other dogs at bay.

"The carpenter's cat is causing all kinds of trouble," Samson told Bummer as Bummer squeezed his way through the throng. "Amundsen is almost beside himself. He nearly had her a second ago."

"We have to help her," Bummer said.

"I think the cat can take care of herself," Samson replied. "Although she is very much outnumbered."

Bummer watched helplessly as Amundsen, who was in a rage after being outsmarted by a cat, cornered Mrs. Chippy. She leaped off the edge of the boat and onto the canvas cover of one of the lifeboats. It swayed as she landed, and for a brief moment it looked as though she was safe. But then she lost her grip and slid off the end.

Bummer jostled his way through the crowd, jumping onto a stack of crates to peer down into the water, despite the fact that his legs felt like jelly and the contents of his stomach were threatening to make an appearance at any moment.

He scanned the churning ocean. There was no sign of the cat anywhere. He didn't know much about cats, but he did know they hated water. He barked to get the attention of the men, but they were too occupied with chasing the dogs around the deck and chaining them back to their kennels.

There! A flash of a paw and a head bobbed in the water.

He barked at Mrs. Chippy, but she didn't hear him at first, too consumed by her terror of the water and her desperate effort to stay afloat. She yowled as a tall wave washed over her, dragging her under. Bummer held his breath and, without thinking, jumped, landing with a heavy splash in the frigid water. His breath was forced out of his lungs as the cold hit him. In his shock, he forgot to swim, and his head sank beneath the water. He cried out, choking on a mouthful of salt water, and paddled as hard as he could to lift his head above the churning surface.

A wave hit him full in the face as he emerged, but he forced his legs to keep moving, keeping his nose high above the water to catch his breath. Another wave washed over him as he swam. His head sank beneath the surface again and he spotted a brown blur a little way ahead. He swam harder toward the blur, grabbing the back of Mrs. Chippy's neck in his mouth when he finally reached her.

"That...is quite...unnecessary!" Mrs. Chippy spluttered, thrashing about while Bummer half swam, half dragged himself and the cat back toward the ship. They'd finally been spotted, and the carpenter had jumped into the water and was heading right for them.

"I can let you go, if you'd like," Bummer mumbled through a mouthful of fur.

Mrs. Chippy shook her head quickly. "This will have to do," she said, adding an almost inaudible "Thank you" beneath her breath.

They were pulled out of the water by some of the crew, and while Mrs. Chippy was whisked away by her human to be dried off, Bummer was left alone to shake the dripping water from his fur.

"I told you!" an excited voice rang out. "Didn't I tell you Bummer was the one you'd want on your team?"

Samson beamed as he and some of the other dogs came over to greet Bummer.

"That was very brave," Sally told him.

Bummer felt his face grow warm. He was about to say that it wasn't such a big deal when a shadow fell over them and the dogs froze.

"Well, now," Shackleton said, reaching down to stroke

Bummer's head. "Looks like I was right about you after all."

Bummer watched with his mouth hanging open as the boss wandered away down the deck.

"Did you hear that, Amundsen?" Samson barked.

Bummer wasn't sure that Amundsen had actually heard what Shackleton had said, but it didn't matter. If the boss believed in him, Bummer thought, maybe it wouldn't be so wrong to believe in himself a little more.

CHAPTER 4

SAMSON

October 1914 to December 1914

They sailed first to Buenos Aires for more supplies, then to Grytviken whaling station, which smelled like fish guts and blubber. The temperature had dropped a few days into sailing across the Weddell Sea, where they had been confronted with pack ice. As they neared Antarctica, it formed on top of the waves, moving with the tides, becoming thicker and thicker, joining to create large rafts of ice called floes. The ship had slowed its course as the ocean seemed to crust over and freeze. The pack ice spread out for endless mile upon mile with only dark, narrow waterways breaking up the blank slate like blue veins across a pale face, creating a mazelike effect.

Samson looked out over the side of the ship, trying to spot the best channels, only to see them converge into a dead end farther along the route.

Often, the ship was accompanied by a pod of humpback whales. They drifted alongside the *Endurance* as the ship sailed, calling out with their mournful song, in a strange language Samson didn't recognize. He tried to reply, but his calls went unanswered.

Swarms of seals and penguins lazed around on top of the ice floes as they passed, sliding into the water on their bellies to search for fish beneath the solid shelves of ice. Samson didn't bother trying to communicate with them. He knew by now that those animals didn't speak. The only thing they were good for was eating.

The *Endurance* had already traveled hundreds of miles, but Captain Worsley said they had at least two hundred and fifty more miles to go until they reached land. The ice surrounding them was so thick that it seemed to Samson as if they were already sailing across the land rather than on an ice-covered ocean.

The ice constantly shifted, making their passage even slower. They navigated into what seemed like a long run of open water, only to find a few miles later that the ice had closed in on them, blocking their path. Samson worried that there might come a time when they became trapped completely, but the ship's specially made bow drove through the ice as the captain sailed at half speed, carving out a V shape in the pack, then drove into it again with the steam engine at full speed to break the ice apart.

Despite their slow progress, Samson loved being out on the open water with the sea breeze ruffling his fur. If he stood on the bow and closed his eyes, it felt as if he were flying, soaring over the waves like an albatross, free to go in whichever direction adventure called him.

"I can feel every single wave," Bummer groaned. "How long until we reach solid land again? Or at least something that resembles solid land. A large rock—or even better, a tropical desert island."

"I thought you'd gotten over your seasickness after your daring rescue of Mrs. Chippy," Samson teased.

Bummer gave him a withering look. Some of the dogs, Samson included, had developed a newfound respect for Bummer since that day. Bummer had taken him by surprise when he'd leaped off the ship. Samson had felt a small burst of pride (once he knew for certain that Bummer hadn't been foolishly trying to abandon ship) as well as feeling a tiny bit smug that he'd been right all along about Bummer.

"We'll be in Antarctica soon enough," Samson said. "That's when the fun will really start. Oh, here comes the boss!"

Samson wagged his tail as Shackleton came over and let him off his chain. He had taken a bit of a liking to Samson and often let Samson keep him company in his quarters while he worked away, looking at plans and drawing and redrawing maps of the route they would take. Samson relished those moments. He wanted to learn as much as he could from the great explorer.

The boss led him belowdecks, and Samson listened to the usual sounds of the crew at work. As they passed by various parts of the ship, Shackleton chatted with Samson, telling him the names of the crew and what their roles were—the seamen working around the boat, the scientists writing in their journals and organizing their instruments, the photographer and artist documenting the journey in paint or on film. Samson was fascinated by Hurley, the photographer, who seemed to be fearless and not as bothered by their situation as the rest of the men. Samson watched as the man climbed with his large box camera up to the very top of the masts, or hung from the tip of the jib boom—the long wooden column that protruded horizontally out over the water.

As they headed along the walkway, Samson paused, sniffing at a closed closet door.

"Come on, old boy!" the boss called.

Samson held firm, snuffling around the edges of the door. He'd caught the scent of something that wasn't quite right. He bent low, growling at the door, then barked loudly. Shackleton placed a finger over his lips to shush Samson, then he gripped the door handle, pulling it open swiftly. There was a sudden yell and bang and out tumbled a red-faced, rather sweaty human, followed by a jumble of spare clothes that landed on top of the man in a heap.

"What do we have here?" the boss boomed with a face like thunder.

"A stowaway!" Samson barked, backing up slightly. He'd never seen the boss look so angry. Samson growled at the stowaway, preparing to grab him by the ankle at the boss's command.

"Up you get!" the boss ordered, hauling the man up by the back of his shirt.

The man stood unsteadily, his eyes wide and hands trembling as the boss marched him into his quarters, slamming the door behind them. Some of the crew gathered around, drawn by the shouts and yells coming from behind the closed door, and then the quivery, pleading voice of the stowaway. Samson suddenly felt a bit sorry for the stowaway. Perhaps he'd just wanted an adventure, too?

"That's enough," Shackleton's second-in-command, Wild, said, coming to see what the fuss was about. "Back to work."

He dragged Samson back up to the top deck. Samson pulled against his collar, whining in frustration. He didn't want to miss out on the drama. He momentarily wondered if the stowaway would be forced to walk the plank as in the pirate stories his old master used to tell the children. Not that the *Endurance* had a plank. Maybe the boss would just drop the stowaway off on the ice?

"I found a stowaway!" Samson told Bummer. "In one of the clothes lockers. The boss was mightily angry."

Bummer frowned at him doubtfully. "Where did a stowaway come from?"

"Maybe Plymouth or when we docked at Buenos Aires—there were plenty of times that a stowaway could have sneaked on board. I'm surprised you didn't hear the boss yelling. I bet he's going to come up here and throw him overboard any moment now."

Samson and Bummer stared expectantly toward the stairwell, but no one appeared. After a while Bummer sighed and lay back down.

"Maybe he's keeping him prisoner for now," Samson said. "To throw him overboard when everyone's asleep so as not to upset the other humans. Oh, there he is!" Samson barked as the stowaway and the boss appeared on deck.

"Do you know that we often get very hungry on these expeditions?" the boss asked the stowaway loudly.

The stowaway nodded.

"And if there is a stowaway available, he is the first to be eaten?" the boss continued.

Samson glanced at Bummer, whose eyes were as wide as his own.

The stowaway froze for a moment, and Samson

thought he might be thinking of making a run for it, but he replied with a grin: "They'd get a lot more meat off you, sir."

The corner of the boss's mouth twitched as he tried not to laugh. "Wild," he said loudly. "Take Blackborow here to meet the cook. The rest of you, prepare the dogs for some exercise."

"You don't think he's really going to eat him?" Bummer squeaked.

Samson shook his head slowly. The boss was a strict man, but he wasn't a monster. Still, Samson could barely hide his relief when Wild returned with Blackborow a few minutes later and introduced him to the rest of the crew as the new steward. Then he suddenly realized what the boss had just said.

"Bummer! They're going to let us off." He paced up and down, his tail wagging as he waited for the men to unleash the dogs.

Bummer looked out at the slowly shifting pack ice uncertainly. "Let us off? Off where?"

Samson grinned and nodded over the side of the ship. "The ice is thick and the floes large enough so that we can finally stretch our legs. I've been dreaming about running for weeks now. Think of it, Bummer, the chill air in your lungs, the ice beneath your paws."

"I don't think you've got much of a choice," Sally said, joining them. "The men want to stretch their legs as much as we do."

The men unhooked their chains, each taking four or five dogs, barely able to hold them all in one place as they bounced up and down with the same eagerness as Samson, desperate to get off the ship.

A steep wooden walkway had been lowered from the deck down onto the ice. Samson raced down, his paws slipping and sliding across the ice, white puffs of air bursting from his jaws as he whooped with joy. He looked back to the ship, where Bummer stood frozen at the top of the gangplank.

"Come on, Bummer!" Samson called out. "It's perfectly safe."

Bummer began a slow trot, stepping as lightly as he could.

"See!" Samson laughed as Bummer caught up with him and Sally.

A thrill ran through Samson as he ran faster, feeling the strength return to his weak muscles and the air filling his lungs. It had been so long since he'd run like this, putting everything else out of his mind except placing one paw in front of the other, that he'd forgotten how exhilarating it could be.

Sally slowed beside him, gesturing ahead. "This doesn't look good."

Samson's stomach tightened. Amundsen, Wolf, and Hercules circled a group of dogs, their teeth bared.

"What are they doing?" Bummer asked, puffing and panting as he caught up.

"Looks like a fight is about to break out," Sally replied. "It was bound to happen sooner or later after being on the ship for so long. We'd best stay out of it."

They had turned to walk back toward the ship and the men, who were having some fun of their own, slipping and sliding over the ice, when the barking started.

Amundsen launched himself at another dog, going for his throat. The other dogs immediately joined in, using their jaws and claws to bite and scratch, slamming their huge bodies into each other.

"The ice is bad," Bummer said. "That dark patch means that it isn't as thick in that spot. They could fall through."

Samson looked at the ice and, sure enough, spotted a darker patch of ice directly behind the fighting dogs.

"We should warn them," he said.

"Wait!" Bummer called out behind him. "It's not safe."

But Samson was already halfway across the ice, watching the dogs edge closer and closer to danger.

Amundsen turned and saw Samson hurtling toward him. Samson tried to bark out a warning about the ice, but before he could, Amundsen leaped into the air, meeting Samson in a tumble of fur and limbs, and they rolled together, sliding to a stop right on top of the blackening ice. There was a loud crack, and both dogs froze as small fissures snaked across the ice, creeping toward them.

"Don't move!" Sally called out, but Amundsen jumped to his feet.

There was a sickening splintering sound as the ice broke up and the ground disappeared suddenly beneath them, pitching Samson and Amundsen into the freezing, churning ocean below. Samson's breath left his lungs as the cold hit, unlike anything he had ever experienced before. He felt as if he were moving in slow motion as he tried to paddle, sinking lower and lower into the water.

The other dogs backed away. Some ran toward the ship, barking.

"Get help!" Samson heard Bummer shout before instructing Sally to take his tail.

Samson could only watch as Bummer slowly edged forward inch by inch, his body low to get as close to the gaping hole as possible.

Samson felt himself slip farther under and lifted his nose as high as he could so that he could breathe.

"Hold on!" Bummer yelled as Sally gripped his tail in her jaws.

"I'm...trying!" Samson gasped, feeling himself slip farther and farther away.

Bummer stretched out his front paws, and Samson reached with his frozen paws to hold on with his claws, slowly pulling himself out of the water with Bummer's help. Just as he was halfway out, he felt an immense weight on his back, forcing him downward to swallow a mouthful of water as Amundsen climbed up and over him onto solid ground.

Samson gasped, his lungs straining as he struggled to

get his head above water, his icy fur weighing him down. He saw the ice beneath Bummer begin to give way as Bummer desperately tried to reach him.

"Amundsen!" Sally growled.

"I can't hold on much longer!" Samson cried.

Sally crouched beside Bummer, holding out her own paws as Amundsen joined her and did the same on the other side. Samson tried to grip them as best he could with his painful, throbbing paws, slowly easing himself up and out of the water.

"You almost drowned me!" Samson gasped, collapsing on the ice. His teeth chattered as he shook his fur as hard as he could. Tiny droplets of ice had formed on the ends of his fur. A fire burned through him suddenly and he leaped up, shoving Amundsen, hard.

"You attacked *me*," Amundsen growled in reply as the two dogs circled each other.

"I didn't attack you," Samson barked. "I was trying to warn you."

Some of the dogs were running toward them across the ice, with the men close behind calling for Amundsen and Samson to stand down, but neither did. Samson glared at Amundsen as he glared right back, neither of them blinking.

"It's true," Sally told Amundsen gently. "He was just trying to warn you."

Amundsen opened his mouth but then snapped his jaws shut again.

"Well," he said finally, his eyes still firmly fixed on Samson.

"Well?" Samson said.

The two glared at each other, neither one wanting to be the first to back down, their hot breath mingling in the air in tiny clouds.

"Amundsen!" Wild called.

Amundsen flinched but didn't move.

The boss whistled. "Samson!"

Samson paused, torn between losing face and being the first to back down, and defying his master. He dragged himself away from Amundsen and trotted over to the boss.

"Good boy," Shackleton said, using a blanket to rub down Samson's fur as Wild did the same to Amundsen. Samson narrowed his eyes at Amundsen, who growled in reply.

CHAPTER 5
SAMSON

January 1915

Samson preferred to sleep on the snow-covered deck rather than inside his stuffy kennel. At night, the sky was so clear that he could see a billion stars twinkling. The tiny ice crystals covering the ship seemed to shimmer back in response. The cool wind and the way the soft snowflakes tingled when they landed on Samson's fur made him feel as if he were back home in Canada. The freezing temperatures didn't bother him. His fur had grown thicker, with a soft, warm underlayer that kept him feeling cozy in the harshest of blizzards.

The boss stood at the front of the ship, gazing out over the ice ahead of them with a steaming cup of cocoa in his hands. Samson went to join him, and the boss patted him on the head.

"It's not looking good, old boy," Shackleton said with a sigh. "According to my schedule, we should already have reached land by now. But with all this ice closing in on us..." He sighed again. "It looks as if we might be stuck here for a while longer."

Samson's stomach lurched as he followed the man's gaze out over the side of the ship. It had already been ten days since they'd become trapped. As they'd moved closer to Antarctica, the passages of ice had become narrower and narrower, until now, with the drop in temperature, they had all but disappeared. The ship was enclosed in the pack ice with no clear passage of water ahead and no way of knowing when they might be able to move again.

Fights broke out every five minutes as the dogs vented their frustration, and the men's moods were just as bad. Often Samson was woken up by a tense argument between the men over some trivial matter. Even Mrs. Chippy hadn't been spotted on deck for weeks, seeming to have the sense to stay out of everyone's way.

Samson nudged Shackleton with his head and tried

to give him a smile. The boss smiled back and nodded to himself as though deciding something. "Well, we might as well make the most of it," he said, downing the last of his cocoa. "There's not much else to do while we're trapped in the ice. So how about we start sled training?"

Samson perked up at this, barked his assent, and ran to tell the others. Bummer didn't seem as enthusiastic as he'd hoped when Samson told him the news.

Bummer's tail drooped slightly. "Do you think ... We will get out of the ice, won't we? We won't be trapped here forever?"

Samson tried to hide his own fear with a small laugh. He'd had the same concern, but there was little he could do about it, and as the boss said—they might as well make the most of their situation. "You've been spending too much time with the scientists," he said. "We just have to wait until the pack ice shifts again, and then we'll be on our way."

I hope, he thought.

Samson pushed past Bummer in his excitement to get off the ship.

Samson joined Sally, waiting as patiently as they could while the men unloaded sleds and harnesses from the ship. Amundsen sauntered over, glaring at Samson. Samson glared back.

"They'll be looking for the leader soon," Amundsen said to Sally, still holding Samson's stare.

"I think we know who will be first choice," Samson replied.

Amundsen narrowed his eyes. "I think we *do*."

Sally looked at them both in turn. "Well, of course we do," she said lightly. "Everyone knows *I'm* the strongest dog here."

Amundsen opened his mouth to argue but snapped his jaws shut again, glaring at Samson before backing away.

"He's got such a big head!" Samson huffed.

"You two are not as dissimilar as you might think." Sally sighed, watching Amundsen leave.

Samson frowned. "Did you forget that he tried to *drown* me?"

"He wasn't trying to drown you. He was trying to save himself. And he did help you...eventually."

Samson grunted. "Only because you asked him to."

Bummer made his way over, his legs slipping on the ice like a newborn deer's. "Steer clear of any dark patches or any areas that look watery," he warned. "And stay away from Amundsen, too."

"Too late for that," Samson mumbled.

They watched the men unload a large sled on skis with an engine and a tall propeller on the back. "Is that the motor sled?" Bummer asked.

"I suppose so," Samson answered. "Although how a machine can be better than a team of dogs who know this kind of terrain is beyond me."

The men whistled and the dogs ran over, eagerly awaiting instructions.

"We'll mix up the teams for now," Shackleton announced, "to see which dogs work well with each other and which can lead."

Samson's tail wagged excitedly. He had to be chosen for leader, he just *had* to. He glanced over at Amundsen, Wolf, and Hercules, who were obviously all thinking the same thing.

"I want that one," Wild called out, pointing at Samson.

Samson's tail drooped a little—he had been hoping to be chosen by Shackleton—but he was still glad to have been first pick.

"I'll take the beast over there," the second officer,

Crean, told Wild, pointing at Amundsen. "I've seen how he operates. He'll beat yours in a footrace any day."

"Is that so?" Wild asked. "How about we have a little wager?"

Captain Worsley; the ship's surgeon, Dr. Macklin; and McNish, the carpenter, also wanted in on the action, choosing Sally, Wolf, and Hercules, respectively.

Each man harnessed his dog and attached the dog to a sled. Samson stood between Wolf and Hercules, who snarled, trying to intimidate him.

"Is that supposed to scare me?" Samson asked with a chuckle.

"It should," Wolf growled. "You may be the biggest, but Hercules and I are faster. What are you going to do when your precious Shackleton realizes you aren't as great as he thinks?"

Samson scowled. "We'll see," he said, digging his claws into the icy ground.

"*Mush!*" Wild shouted, and Samson was off. He quickly overtook Wolf, but as he passed Hercules, the dog snapped at Samson's tail, catching a mouthful of fur. Samson pressed his claws harder into the ice, throwing up flurries into Hercules's face.

Samson ran faster, until he was head-to-head with Sally on one side and Amundsen close by on the other.

"*Gee!*" Wild shouted, the signal to turn right. Samson veered to the right, strengthening his lead over Amundsen. Sally was still close on his tail, though, changing her position to take the inside.

"*Haw!*" Wild shouted. Samson merged to the left, trying to cut in front of Sally, but she swerved, cutting him off. Amundsen was hot on their tails as they headed to the finish line, where men and dogs cheered them on. Samson gave it everything he had, even though his legs burned and his muscles trembled with the effort. At the last minute, Sally came out of nowhere with a burst of speed, beating him to the post.

"*Whoa!*" Wild shouted as Samson skidded to a halt, slumping to the ground.

Amundsen landed beside him, the two dogs panting hard to regain their breath.

"See?" puffed Sally above them. "I told you I was the best."

A loud whistle sounded, cutting through the excitement, and men and dogs turned to the ship. Steam had begun rising from the funnel. The fires had been put out days ago, partly because the ship had nowhere to go and partly, Samson guessed, to preserve fuel.

"Are we on the move?" Bummer asked, racing alongside Samson, eager to return to the ship.

"I hope so," Samson said, disappointed that training had been cut short but glad that they were on their way. Although Shackleton remained his optimistic self, Samson had heard whispers from the crew about what would happen if they were trapped. Samson had tried to put it out of his mind, but he couldn't help worrying about what they would do next. What if they ran out of food or were unable to call for help? Did anyone in the outside world even know where they were?

Dogs and men boarded quickly as the steam rose thicker and faster into the sky, the men looking happier than they had in weeks. There was a loud groan as the ship tried to break free from the icy grasp that held it. Samson looked over the bow. A little way ahead, a narrow passage of water opened up as the pressure of the ship against the ice disturbed the floe, breaking it apart. Samson ran down to the boss, barking at him until he spotted the lead, desperate for the ship to get moving.

"Passage ahead!" the boss called out.

The steam slowed, and the men hurried back out onto the ice, carrying with them chisels, picks, saws, anything they could use to break up the ice and widen the lead of water. Samson wished they would let him back out onto the ice. He could help the men by pulling ropes or...something. But the dogs were forced to remain on board, so all Samson could do was watch helplessly as the men toiled, attacking the ice with their tools and hauling away huge chunks of ice from the water, then breaking them up. The ship lurched forward suddenly, moving ahead a few feet, and both dogs and men gave a cheer in triumph, but the small victory was short-lived.

As day turned into night, then back to morning, the men seemed to be fighting a losing battle. The passage of water wasn't any wider. As soon as the men cut away the ice surrounding the ship, more ice quickly replaced it.

Ahead, tantalizingly close, lay open water. But between that and the *Endurance* lay four hundred yards of thick, immovable ice. Eventually, the boss signaled for the men to put down their tools. One by one, the defeated, exhausted men returned to the ship.

Men and dogs gathered around Shackleton as they waited to hear what they would do next. Samson's stomach churned, but he felt sure that the boss would have a plan. There was no reason to think they would be trapped forever. It was a minor setback, nothing more.

"The ship seems stuck fast," Shackleton said. "So for now, we wait and hope that when the weather warms we can continue the journey."

"Can we call for help?" one of the crew shouted out.

Shackleton glanced at the captain and shook his head.

"We're too far out of range to contact anyone by radio. Maybe as the ice floe shifts, we might move closer to land...." Shackleton drifted off, unable to give them any better news.

"I guess that's it, then," Samson said, returning to his kennel for the first time in weeks, feeling as defeated as the men.

"Maybe not," said Sally, coming to join them. "I have to believe that we'll return home one day...that I'll see my mate again."

"We can't be that far away from land," Samson said. "Maybe we will move closer to land as the captain said?"

"We're not that far from land," Bummer said. "*If the ocean were clear, and the pack ice not in our way...*

But now that we're stuck, we're drifting *away* from the Antarctic."

Samson shook his head hard. That couldn't be it, could it? They couldn't have come so far only to get stuck in the ice to drift without ever making it to land. Without ever having started the expedition.

"There has to be something the boss can do? Some way?" Samson asked desperately.

Bummer sighed. "There's nothing to do now but wait."

CHAPTER 6

BUMMER

February 1915

The ship drifted along on the ice floe, moving farther and farther away from the land that had been so close. Bummer couldn't help feeling all hope ebb away with it.

The boss called a halt to their routine and decided to move the dogs off the ship, which was now permanently entrenched in the ice, and onto the floe. The ship was turned into a makeshift camp for the men that they named the Ritz, after the famous hotel.

Some of the men set to work constructing kennels on the ice with McNish. First they built up the snow into dog-sized igloos, then used spare pieces of wood to reinforce the openings so that the snow wouldn't cave in. They added a hospital and quarantine ward for sick dogs, and an outdoor stove, which the men gathered around during the day and the dogs at night when the humans were on the ship.

"How do you like dog town?" Samson asked, checking out Bummer's kennel-igloo.

"It's not so bad," Bummer said, grateful to finally have a space of his own without being constantly surrounded by dogs. The men had added sacks filled with straw for beds, and it was the most comfortable Bummer had felt since they'd set sail. "You know, they should call these kennels *dogloos* because they are igloos for dogs."

Samson laughed. "Come on, the boss is about to choose the team leaders."

"I won't be chosen," Bummer replied sullenly, following Samson toward the ship.

"You have just as good a chance as me," Samson said.

Bummer stopped and stared at him until Samson conceded, "Well, maybe you won't be chosen as sled leader, but I'm sure *I* will and you can be on my team."

Bummer perked up at this. Pulling a sled might be fun if he was with his friends. It would beat being stuck on the ship, at least. They reached the crowd of men and dogs. The boss had already begun pairing up each of the men with his own team of dogs. Every single member of the expedition would be in charge of at least three dogs.

"Wild!" Shackleton called out, reading from a piece of paper in his hand.

Wild stepped forward.

"Your sled leader is Samson, with Sally, Gruss, Bob, Jasper, Saint, Tim, and Surly."

Samson turned to look at Bummer, his eyebrows knitted together in a deep frown. "Sorry," he mouthed, joining Wild and the rest of his team. "Maybe you'll be with Mack," he called back. "He's a good sport."

Bummer sat patiently, waiting for his name to be called, a feeling of unease growing in his belly as more dogs joined their teams. He glanced around to see who was left. There weren't many. Only Amundsen, Wolf, Hercules, and a few other dogs whom Bummer hadn't had the chance to get to know. His gut twisted as he realized that they were the final team.

"Crean," the boss announced.

Bummer hesitated. Crean was kind enough—maybe it wouldn't be so bad if he was in charge.

"Your team leader is Amundsen, with Wolf, Hercules, Satan, Rufus, Judge, Noel, and..." He paused to glance over at the remaining dogs. "Bummer."

Wolf and Hercules groaned as Bummer's name was called out. Bummer felt as if his body and limbs were weighed down with the dread of being on Amundsen's team.

"I'm doomed," he whispered to Samson and Sally.

"I'm sure it won't be as bad as you think," Sally said, but Samson gave Bummer a grim look that said he thought otherwise.

"Maybe they will switch the teams around when we reach land?" Samson said, trying to lift his spirits.

"*If* we ever reach land," Bummer mumbled as he was harnessed up by Crean.

Crean worked them all day and well into the evening, racing them back and forth while he rode on the sled, yelling out commands, seemingly having the time of his life. It took Bummer a while to get used to the pull of the harness: the way it rubbed and chafed his skin, and the constant urge to scratch beneath it. His discomfort was soon forgotten after Amundsen snarled at Bummer when he put a foot wrong...or was too slow...or in the way...or turned in the wrong direction.

"Don't listen to him, lad," Judge puffed beside him. "You're doing a good job."

Bummer tried to smile, but he barely had the energy to breathe. Finally, Crean drove them back to camp, where many of the other dogs were settled in their dog-loos for the evening. Bummer searched for Samson, finding him playing with a ball on the ice with the humans and a few other dogs. The men had set up two poles on either side of a large expanse of ice, and the aim of the game seemed to be to get the ball between the two poles.

"Bummer!" Samson called. "Come and join us. The humans call it football."

Bummer paused. He couldn't quite see the point of it, and all he really wanted to do was eat his meal and settle in front of the stove for the evening to warm his aching bones, but he hadn't seen Samson all day, so he ran over to join them.

"You can be on Surly's team," Samson told him. "All you have to do is get the ball and run it past my team and between the poles. Simple!"

Simple? Bummer thought. It was simple enough for Samson, who could outrun the wind, but not for him. More dogs came over to watch the game, including Amundsen and Sally. Bummer ran as fast as he could, chasing after the ball, but only managed to get even slightly close when the other team was heading toward him. As they scored yet another goal, Bummer stopped to catch his breath.

"Bummer!" Sally shouted from the sidelines. Bummer looked up, startled to see Samson heading right for him. He ran forward to intercept the ball but lost his courage at the last minute as Samson barreled toward him. Bummer gave chase, feeling a surge in energy as Sally and some of the others cheered him on.

Samson stumbled ahead, faltering. His front leg had slipped down into the snow and he was stuck fast. Bummer ran faster, joy swelling in his chest as he took the ball right from under Samson's nose and ran it between the poles.

The dogs and men cheered, and even Samson whooped from the other end of the field. Bummer glanced over to the sidelines to see Amundsen watching him closely; then, to Bummer's surprise, Amundsen gave him a small smile before wandering away to his dogloo.

That night, a blizzard blew into camp, covering the entrance to Bummer's dogloo with snow. He pushed out a paw, poking a hole in the snow so that he could breathe, then tried to settle down to sleep.

He opened his eyes again with a start and heard a cry on the wind from one of the dogloos. He clawed at the snow to make a hole big enough to fit through, then hurried around dog town, barely able to see more than a few paws ahead as the blizzard swirled snow all around him. Bummer's ears pricked up as he searched for the source of the noise. Whoever it was sounded as if they were in pain. He kept his eyes closed against the biting wind, following the sound to Sally's dogloo, where Amundsen paced nervously at the entrance.

"What's happening?" Bummer whispered, worried that Amundsen had hurt her. "Sally, are you all right?"

Sally looked up at Bummer, her eyes wide as she let out another agonizing cry.

"I tried to get help," Amundsen said. "But the blizzard...I couldn't find my way to the ship."

"Wait there!" Bummer cried. "I'll get help."

Amundsen called after him, but the words were lost on the wind. He raced to Samson's dogloo to wake him.

"It's Sally," Bummer gasped.

Samson raced out of his dogloo and Bummer chased

after, losing sight of him in the blizzard a few times as his legs, still aching from the day's training, struggled to keep up.

"What have you done to her?" Samson snarled at Amundsen.

"He hasn't done anything," Sally panted as she caught her breath. "He's trying to help."

"If I stay here with Sally, can you go and wake Dr. Macklin?" Samson asked. "I don't want to leave her with Amundsen." Macklin was a surgeon for the men, but as they had no veterinarian, he also served as doctor to the dogs for anything that couldn't be dealt with by the crew.

Bummer didn't wait to be told twice; he pushed his way through the snow. His eyes watered as the harsh wind cut into them. He kept his head low, squinting through the blizzard for any sign of the ship. A few times, he was blown off course by the heavy wind and driving snow, losing his footing as he fought a battle against nature itself, pushing against it to reach someone who could help Sally. Finally, he saw the dull glow of an oil lantern and raced toward it, scrabbling up the gangplank and down into the main part of the ship where the men slept. In the darkness the men all looked the same in their bunks, so he barked loudly to wake them.

Crean was the first to wake. "I think he's trying to tell us something," he said, pulling on his fur gloves and boots.

Bummer didn't wait for him to follow—he hurried back to Sally, the wind now at his back, urging him on.

"The men are coming," Bummer panted.

Samson turned around and smiled. "She's going to be fine, Bummer," he whispered. "Look!"

Bummer peered over Samson's shoulder. Sally lay on her side, looking as exhausted as Bummer felt, with four tiny wet bundles of fur snuggling against her.

"Pups!" Bummer gasped as the one closest raised its tiny pink nose to sniff the air.

"Bummer," Sally said, "meet Nell, Nelson, Roger, and Toby."

Bummer beamed down at the tiny creatures, amazed at the wonder of life.

"I wish their father were here to see them," she whispered.

"Is he still in Canada?" Bummer asked.

Sally nodded. "I didn't know I was expecting pups

until it was too late. Now he might never meet them." She sniffed, licking each pup on its head in turn.

The men finally caught up, as surprised as Bummer to see the newborn puppies.

"We'll get home," Bummer told her. "Somehow, we'll get there."

CHAPTER 7
SAMSON

May 1915

Samson hadn't quite understood the part in Shackleton's advertisement where it had mentioned long months of complete darkness. The only words he had really remembered were *honor and recognition*, but now that the sun no longer rose in the morning and the days were filled with endless night, the other parts were slowly coming back to him. He thought for a moment of asking Bummer to remind him what else the advertisement had warned about, but he wasn't sure he really wanted to know the answer.

At least now that the boss had decided they had no choice but to wait out the dark months of the Antarctic winter, the dogs weren't kept captive on board the ship. Each day, Samson led his team across the ice. Surly, as his name suggested, was less enthusiastic than the others but fell in line quickly enough when Samson barked out his orders. They were one of the fastest sled teams.

Samson glanced over to where Crean was setting up Amundsen and his team in their harnesses on the floe, ready for another day of hunting, exploring, and fishing. To make their food rations last longer, they brought back penguins and seals, using their blubber as fuel for the stove and their meat for food. Bummer stood in the back of the group looking a sorry state. He was at least a head smaller than the other dogs.

Bummer gave Samson a half-smile, half-grimace as Crean put on his harness.

"Stop pulling at the harness!" Amundsen snapped at Bummer as he was pulled suddenly to one side by Bummer's anxious bouncing.

"I wish Bummer were on our team," Sally sighed behind Samson, watching as Amundsen's team set off with Bummer's legs moving twice as fast just to keep pace with the others. Occasionally he stumbled, and Judge would nudge him onward before Amundsen could notice and snap at him again.

Roger snuggled up to his mother. "Couldn't he stay behind with us?" he asked.

Nelson nodded. "If Bummer doesn't want to pull the sled, why does he have to go? He could play with us instead."

Sally smiled as Toby tried to climb up onto her back. "Your father has a rule—no dog left behind. When he was out with his sled team back home, it didn't matter if he wanted to keep going—if any of his team needed a rest or was injured, the rest of the team would help. Bummer might be smaller and slower than the rest of his team, but they will help him if he needs it. That's what a team does."

"Just like us!" Nell said.

Sally laughed. "Exactly."

"I'm not sure Amundsen's heard of that rule," Samson muttered under his breath.

"I asked Amundsen to go easy on Bummer," Sally whispered back as Wild tightened the harnesses around Samson's shoulders and beneath his stomach. "I just hope he listened."

Sally said a quick goodbye as she returned to camp with her pups, unable to join her team until she was back to full strength.

"We'll have to stay steady today," Samson said, changing the subject so he wouldn't dwell on his friend's discomfort. "We're one dog short, and the pressure beneath the floes has driven up more obstacles."

The captain said they were drifting north encased in the ice, each day moving farther away from land, so that by the time the ice began to thaw enough for the ship to be freed, they could be hundreds of miles off course. Though the ice was solid and thick, beneath it churned the ocean, dark, wild, and unyielding. The subtle vibrations and pressure below the ice often drove up great mounds and ridges of ice, so Samson had to be careful to make sure he chose the best path—especially since it was harder to see in the perpetual twilight. One wrong turn could mean they'd end up trapped between ridges, or worse—beneath the ice. Samson had learned his lesson when he and Amundsen had been submerged in freezing water, and it wasn't an experience he wanted to repeat anytime soon.

With the dogs fully harnessed, Wild stood on the sled behind them. *"Mush!"*

Samson was keenly aware of each dog on his team, slowing his pace when he sensed one struggling, racing on when he knew they felt the call of the wild and the urge to run. Each time they ran, Samson learned more about his team, and they about him, until they trusted one another completely.

Today there was nothing but wilderness and the wide-open whiteness of it all. Samson thought he could probably run in any direction for days without having to stop. All around them, icebergs rose and fell in the distance, reflecting the bright white of the moon. The ground beneath Samson's feet sparkled like crushed diamonds, and the sky above was a deep purple smear of ink. It was one of the most breathtaking sights Samson had ever seen.

Samson decided to take a diversion from his usual route to see if they could find some thinner ice that Wild could cut through to get to the fish below. As he ran, he felt a small vibration beneath his paws. Nothing big, more of a little tickle that ran through his fur. He slowed slightly, but Wild yelled at him to continue on, so he picked up his pace.

Another tremor came from beneath the ice. A little to his right—pressure forcing two floes together, creating a rising, impenetrable wall. Samson swerved to the left, but another ridge rose beside him.

"*Haw!*" Wild called to Samson to turn, but there was nowhere to go but forward.

"Be ready to change direction at my command," Samson barked at his team.

The dogs barked in reply as they drove on through the rolling landscape, rising up one moment, sinking down the next. It felt to Samson almost as though they were running across ocean waves—each one higher and more dangerous than the last, threatening to crush and drag them into the depths below.

The ridges continued to rise on either side, converging to create a narrowing pathway. Samson's heart thundered hard in his chest as he tried to focus on keeping his team safe.

"Run faster than you have ever run before!" Samson barked.

This time the dogs didn't bark in reply, their breath strained by the effort of running flat out, but Samson felt them behind him, pushing him on as the space ahead became narrower and narrower still.

"Faster!"

The sides of the sled behind him scraped against the ice. Their only point of escape narrowed with every heartbeat. With a final push, they squeaked through a split second before the ridges crashed against each other, closing up the path behind them.

"*Whoa!*" Wild called, his voice shaky.

The dogs slid to a halt, their sides heaving as they panted to catch their breath. The ice creaked and settled around them and the ground fell still beneath Samson's paws.

"I think we'd best head back to the ship," Samson puffed, smiling gratefully at his team. They hadn't let him down for one second.

Wild seemed to agree as the dogs turned back toward the ship via a different route, winding in and out of the new ridges created by the ice shift. As they approached the *Endurance*, they found that many other dog teams had returned and were on the ship.

Samson felt his chest tighten as they neared. "What is it?" he asked Bummer and Sally, a little way ahead.

"The ship," Bummer said, running to meet him. "The ice ridges have moved farther up against the sides."

Samson moved closer. As he watched, ice crept,

almost imperceptibly, up the sides of the hull, as though the *Endurance* was slowly being devoured by a great monster. What would they do if the ship was lost? How would they get home? Sally and her pups might never return to Canada.... They were so small. How would they survive out in the wilderness with their food supply dwindling and no way to reach land?

"What happens to the ship if the ice doesn't thaw?" Samson whispered, although he feared he already knew the answer.

"If the floes keep shifting," Bummer said, "the pressure will likely crush it...."

Samson felt his heart drop. "And then there really will be no way home," he finished.

CHAPTER 8

SAMSON

June 1915

The humans were celebrating something they called Midwinter's Day. Samson didn't really understand what it was all about, but the men decided to have a feast in its honor, which meant the dogs had a feast of their own. Instead of their usual meal of pemmican (a mixture of dried meats), the humans opened up tins of ham and fish, which the dogs gulped down. It wasn't that pemmican was so bad, but when Samson had eaten the same meal day after day with little change in his diet other than the infrequent seal steak or piece of blubber, finally tasting something new was heaven.

The days were becoming dull. Even taking the sled

out on the ice lost its appeal after a while. The constant twilight didn't help matters. Often Samson felt that his mood would only lift when the sun rose in the sky again and thawed the ice so that the *Endurance* would finally be free. The men had done the best they could to hack away at it to stop the ice from moving any farther, but the threat was always there, and no matter how carefree the men tried to appear, Samson knew that they were as worried as he was about the fate of the ship.

The moon was especially bright that night, seeming to light a path before Samson, giving him an idea to lift the dogs' mood.

"Who's up for a race?" Samson asked, wandering from one dogloo to the next, avoiding those belonging to the less amenable dogs.

"What kind of race?" Bummer asked, peering out from his dogloo.

Samson grinned. "Come with me and you'll find out."

He moved far enough from the ship that they wouldn't wake the sleeping men, then waited for the dogs to assemble and explained what he had in mind.

"Welcome to the first annual Twilight Antarctic

Derby!" Samson announced, to puzzled looks from the dogs crowding around.

Samson sighed. "It's a dog race," he explained. "Sled teams will race two at a time, with full harnesses and sleds. The winners of each round will be pitted against each other until the final, where we'll find out which team among us is the best. Who's in?" he asked.

There was an awkward silence for a moment; then, to Samson's surprise, Surly stepped forward with a rare smile. "I'm in," he said.

"Bummer?" Samson asked. "How about it?"

Bummer looked around uncertainly. "My sled team isn't here," he said. "I can't race by myself. Also...how will we put on the harnesses without the humans' help?"

"Ah, good point," Samson replied. "We can step into the harnesses; they just won't be as tight as usual."

"You can take my place," Sally said. "I need to watch the pups, and it will give the rest of you a fairer chance."

Bummer grinned and bounded over to Surly and the rest of the team.

More dogs followed, standing in their usual team formations with the leaders at the head of the pack, waiting for Samson's instructions.

"We race two teams at a time," Samson repeated. He nodded ahead to a line of tall ice mounds that the men had set up with ropes and lanterns on top in case anyone lost his way back to the ship in the darkness. "To the end of the ice mounds, circle around, then back here to the finish line. The rules are: No fighting or obstructing the other team—we want a clean race. No dirty tricks to get ahead. Understand?"

The dogs barked in agreement, and the first two teams slipped into their harnesses, then lined up at the starting line, which Bummer had dug out with his claws.

"Ready?" Samson asked the team leaders, Spider and Mack. The dogs nodded, digging their claws into the ice to ensure a quick start.

"You weren't planning on starting without us, were you?" a low voice came from the back of the crowd.

Samson froze as Amundsen, Wolf, and Hercules pushed their way past the dogs to face him. "Just because you're the boss's favorite, that doesn't make you the boss of us dogs."

"You're welcome to join in," Samson said lightly, pretending that he hadn't left them out on purpose. "But we don't want any foul play. If you want to race to win, you have to do it fair and square."

Amundsen took a step back, offended. "Of course! What do you take us for?"

Bummer reluctantly joined them, and Samson gave him an apologetic look. He knew Bummer had only agreed to the race because he thought he'd be on Samson's team. Samson hoped Amundsen wouldn't make Bummer look like a fool in front of the other dogs just to prove a point.

He turned to the dogs waiting impatiently at the starting line. "Ready?" he asked again.

The dogs gave a brief nod, focusing on the path ahead.

"Mush!"

With a scraping of claws on ice and a blur of fur, they were off. The two teams were fairly evenly matched, with only a head's difference as they quickly reached the end of the line of ice mounds and navigated their sleds around, thundering back toward the finish line.

There was barely a paw length between them as they crossed the line, skidding to a stop in a jumble of limbs and harnesses.

"Spider's team won this round," Samson announced. "But only by a nose. Next to race is—"

"We'll go next," Amundsen declared.

Samson was about to protest, but Amundsen glared at any dog who looked as if they wanted to disagree, and they lowered their heads, suddenly more interested in the ice at their feet than in racing.

"All right," Samson said after a pause. "You can race—"

"We'll race your team," Amundsen said, cutting Samson off again. "That's if you're up for the challenge?"

Surly growled and nodded his assent to Samson.

Bummer shook his head almost imperceptibly at Samson, but what choice did Samson have? He couldn't turn down a challenge from Amundsen. It would show that he accepted Amundsen as his alpha, and Samson would never do that, no matter what was at stake. Besides, he thought, it was only a simple race around the track. What harm could it do? Samson knew they had the advantage over Amundsen's team with Bummer taking the rear. He immediately felt guilty about the thought and pushed it out of his mind as he lined up in front of his team beside Amundsen. Each dog strained at the harness, ready to go. Samson realized suddenly that there was much more at stake than a simple race. This was about who was the better dog.

"Go, Samson!" Nell shouted as Sally and her pups came to watch.

Samson gave the tiny light gray pup a grin.

Mack took Samson's place as race starter, and an eerie hush fell over the crowd.

"Go, Amundsen!" Nelson yelled even more loudly than his sister.

Samson frowned at the tiny pup, then at Sally, who shrugged with a smile.

"And Bummer," Nelson added, slightly less loudly.

Amundsen studied the little pup bouncing up and down excitedly. He glanced over at Samson and grinned. "They have no chance against my team," he told Nelson, who exploded into a series of whoops and howls.

"Ready?" Mack asked.

Samson nodded, glancing at Amundsen out of the corner of his eye, then focusing on the track ahead.

"*Mush!*" Mack shouted.

Samson ran harder than he had ever run in his life. He felt the pull of the slower dogs behind him and the drag of the sled across the bumpy terrain, but he kept his pace. He was going to win this race no matter what—even if it meant dragging his entire team over the finish line. As they reached the end of the ice mounds, he slowed, preparing to take the sharp turn, but Amundsen kept his pace, not slowing for a second.

They're going to crash! Samson thought, keeping one eye ahead and one eye on Amundsen's team, with Bummer barely managing to keep up, his breath and legs straining. As Samson's team turned smoothly, Amundsen's swung out much too fast, sending the sled tumbling over the ice, entangling Bummer and his loose harness with it. Samson slowed, glancing back at his friend.

"Keep going!" Surly yelled.

Samson forced himself to look ahead. He couldn't let his team down. Not when they were so close to the finish line. He'd complete the race, then go back for Bummer. Bummer knew how important it was for him to teach Amundsen a lesson....In fact, Bummer might even be upset if Samson stopped now to return for him. Samson shoved aside the voice in his head that said he was being a bad friend, pushing on to finish the race.

They crossed the line to barks and howls from the

crowd. The dogs surrounded Samson and his team, barking congratulations. None of them particularly liked Amundsen, so Samson's victory felt like a victory for them all.

All except Bummer.

CHAPTER 9

BUMMER

June 1915

Every inch of his body hurt. Bummer tried to move, but he was pinned down by the immense weight of the wooden sled on top of him. His head felt woozy, and his body shook from the shock or cold or both.

Around him he could hear faint voices and barking, but he couldn't distinguish between them.

"Samson," Bummer whined. "Are you there?"

"Bummer!" a deep voice growled close to his ear. "Can you hear me?"

"Samson?" Bummer called again.

"No," the voice barked. "It's Amundsen. Stay still, the other dogs have gone for help."

"Amundsen!" Bummer cried weakly. "My leg. I can't move it."

Bummer heard Amundsen call Wolf and Hercules over. "We have to move the sled," he told them.

"Let's wait for the men," Wolf said.

"Why are you so worried about the runt, anyway?" Hercules argued. "It's his fault we lost the race."

Amundsen growled, then broke off as a small voice called out.

"Amundsen! Is Bummer all right?" Nelson asked. Bummer could hear the quiver in his voice, and he felt even more afraid.

Amundsen made no reply.

Nelson gave a tiny growl. "Mother says you never leave a team dog behind."

"Nelson," Amundsen started, then sighed. "The pup is right," he barked at Wolf and Hercules. "A leader doesn't abandon his team. Help me lift the sled."

The light around the sled shifted. Bummer watched helplessly as the dark, looming shadows of Wolf, Hercules, and Amundsen got into position, Wolf and Hercules at each end and Amundsen taking the brunt of the weight in the center.

The pressure on Bummer's body eased slightly so that he was able to breathe more deeply. Inch by inch, he slowly pulled himself toward the gap that Amundsen had made and squeezed himself out, his injured paw dragging limply along. As soon as his tail was free, Amundsen let out a roar and dropped the sled.

Bummer stood slowly, gingerly moving each of his limbs in turn, then his tail, wincing when he tried to step on his front paw.

"Bummer!" Nelson cried, his little tail wagging as he rubbed against Bummer's side.

Bummer tried to smile. "I'm a little bruised, but I'm sure I'll be fine." He looked around. "Where's Samson?"

"The *hero* of dog town?" Wolf snarled, gesturing with his head behind them.

Bummer turned. Samson was still in the thick of the other dogs, howling and celebrating his victory. Bummer looked at the ground, unable to watch anymore. He turned back to Amundsen, but he was walking away with Wolf and Hercules, his head hung low.

"Amundsen, wait!" Bummer called, limping as fast as he could to catch up, to thank the other dog.

Amundsen paused but didn't turn around. "The pup was right," he growled, glancing over his shoulder at the cheering dogs. "No dog left behind."

CHAPTER 10

BUMMER

July 1915

The wind howled around dog town, sounding to Bummer like ghouls screaming out a warning. In Bummer's head it sounded like: *Turn back! Turn back! Danger ahead!* Bummer buried his head in his paws, trying to block out the sound and hoping his kennel was strong enough to make it through the night. The ice walls were sturdy enough, but the wooden beam at the entrance rattled. Outside, snow and debris were whipped up into miniature tornadoes that swept across the floe. Some of the humans' clothes that they'd hung out to dry flapped past in the wind as though flying away to freedom. Bummer curled his body up tightly, laying his tail over his head and squeezing his eyes shut, trying to sleep until it was all over.

In the morning, he was woken by something he hadn't seen in a long time: the sun, rising over the ice. Its hazy orange glow reflected on the sparkling surface, warm and bright. There were already watery patches around the ship, and it felt as though the arrival of the sun had brought with it the return of hope. Hope that the ice would thaw and the ship would be freed so they could set sail once more.

Dog town seemed to be more or less intact after the blizzard, but Bummer couldn't say the same for the *Endurance*. The ship seemed to have shifted ever so slightly, leaning to one side. The deck was covered with pieces of wood and canvas, crates that had been blown over and covered in a thick coating of snow already turning to slush in the warmth of the sun. He wondered if Mrs. Chippy was all right. He'd gone back onto the ship a few times to invite her to dog town, but she'd declined. He didn't blame her. After the shock of being chased by a group of dogs and ending up in the freezing ocean, he wasn't surprised she wanted to keep her distance.

"Bummer!" Nell called, bounding across the ice toward him, skating more than running. "We're going to learn how to pull a sled! Come and watch!"

Bummer smiled at the tiny pup, so full of energy and joy. The puppies had never known any life other than out here on the ice, and they seemed to be thriving. Bummer wished he felt their enthusiasm.

"Are you sure your mother said that was all right?" Bummer asked, looking around for Sally. "The sled is very heavy."

Toby ran over with his brothers and nodded. "Mother said we're big enough."

"We're a team just like you and Amundsen," Nelson added.

Bummer smothered the urge to correct him. "Well, I suppose you'll have to learn sometime."

He limped after the tiny puppies, who were light gray like their mother, with small tufts of soft white fur beneath.

"Are you ready?" Samson called over, coming out of his dogloo.

Bummer paused. "Samson is teaching you?"

Toby nodded. "He's the fastest dog in camp."

"No, he is not!" Nell huffed. "Mother is."

Roger nodded in agreement with his sister, but Nelson shook his head. "Amundsen is the fastest and the strongest in camp—*everyone* knows that, don't they, Bummer?" he called as he ran off with his brothers.

Bummer nodded, distracted. He hadn't spoken to Samson since the race. Samson had tried to talk to him, but Bummer had turned the other way. He continued to avoid Samson as much as possible, until Samson seemed to have given up. Bummer's leg was almost healed—the wound having been cleaned and bandaged by Crean—but he still held it slightly above the ice as he walked, not wanting to put his full weight on it in case the searing pain returned.

Nell frowned. "Are you coming, Bummer?"

Bummer glanced up at Samson, who was laughing as Roger, Toby, and Nelson playfully snapped their jaws in the air, trying to catch his tail.

"My leg is still feeling sore," Bummer said. "And I just remembered that I have to go out hunting with my team. I should probably stay here and rest."

"Will you watch us for a little while?" Nell asked. "Please!"

"All right," Bummer answered, unable to disappoint the pup. "Just a few minutes."

The puppies stepped into the harnesses on the ground, which were attached to the sled. Bummer tried not to laugh. The harnesses were at least four sizes too big for the pups and hung limply over their shoulders. On Samson's command they pulled together, straining as hard as they could, but the sled stayed put. Roger at the back of the pack stumbled forward, knocking into his brothers and then sweeping Nell's paws from under her as they landed in a tumble of fur.

Bummer couldn't help laughing as the pups struggled to untangle themselves from their harnesses and each other, their small legs flailing in the air as they tried to break free. He caught Samson's eye, then quickly looked away as he remembered the feeling when Samson had left him behind. The pain in his leg wasn't half as bad as the pain in his chest every time he thought about it.

He had turned to leave when he felt a sudden movement beneath his paws.

Ahead, the *Endurance* shifted slightly; then all at once, ice rose up on each side, grinding against the ship like cat's claws. The ice began to crack up all around dog town. Huge blocks of ice were thrown up as floes pushed together, rising up and out of the ocean. The ice blocks crashed down on the dogloos, crushing some while others sank into the deep cracks, disappearing into the black water below.

"Samson!" Bummer called out, racing for the pups. "We have to get back to the ship!"

The men had already started herding as many dogs as they could onto the ship as the floe shifted all around them—rising, then falling. One moment Bummer had to swerve to avoid a wall of ice rising in front of him, then the next he had to leap over a deep crevice as the pack ice split apart. Samson frantically pulled at the ropes of the harnesses with his teeth, but they seemed to have knotted, trapping the pups like fish in a net. Nell, the smallest, managed to wriggle free, and Toby followed, but Nelson and Roger were well and truly stuck.

Bummer reached them, and Nell cowered beneath him as he took the other side of the harness in his jaws. "Pull!" he mumbled to Samson. Samson nodded and the two pulled in opposite directions as hard as they could, making a space big enough for Roger to escape. The pups huddled against Samson, trying to keep their balance as the ice shifted this way and that and Bummer tried to free Nelson.

Suddenly, the ground beneath them cracked and split in two, with Samson and the three pups on one side and Bummer and Nelson on the other. Just as Bummer moved forward to grab hold of Nelson, the ice split again, separating them. Bummer tried to leap across, but his paw wasn't strong enough. The ice rose up between them, creating a wall, hiding Nelson and the sled from view.

"Nelson!" Bummer barked, his heart pounding in his chest as he frantically searched for a way to reach the pup. For all he knew, Nelson was already beneath the floe.

"Nelson!" Bummer shouted again and again until his throat was raw.

There was a roar, and suddenly Amundsen appeared out of nowhere, leaping up and over the ridge with Nelson in his jaws. He landed with a loud thump beside Bummer, and the floe shifted again beneath their feet.

"Nelson! Are you all right?" Bummer asked.

The little pup nodded, his eyes wide and his fur quivering.

"We have to get to the ship!" Bummer yelled over the crash of ice raining down on the floe.

Samson was already halfway to the ship, carrying Nell in his jaws while Toby and Roger clung to his back, wailing for their mother. Bummer and Amundsen followed, leaping from floe to floe, looking out for thin patches of ice. They finally reached the ship, and Crean hurried down to take the pups.

"That was close," Bummer puffed, his eyes wide.

"I didn't think we were going to make it," Amundsen replied.

"Nelson wouldn't have if it hadn't been for you."

Nelson was still clinging to Amundsen's fur, refusing to let go even as Amundsen shook his entire body.

"No dog left behind!" Nelson announced, licking Amundsen behind the ear.

Bummer laughed as Amundsen made a disgusted face and shook the pup off his back, escaping quickly to his kennel before Nelson could follow.

Samson wandered over, and the two stood together for a while in an awkward silence.

"Bummer," Samson said finally. "I'm sorry...about the race. I got so caught up in winning and I didn't want to let my team down...and..." He trailed off.

"I thought *we* were a team," Bummer said. "You knew I was hurt but you left me behind."

"We *are* a team," Samson replied. "But I was so close to the finish line. I couldn't lose a challenge from Amundsen, you know that. I was going to come straight back for you, but..." He trailed off again, looking down at the ground.

Bummer paused for a moment. Part of him wanted to say it was all right, that he forgave Samson, but the other part remembered how he'd felt when Samson left him.

Bummer shook his head, unable to find the right words to say, then limped to his kennel.

CHAPTER 11
SAMSON

August 1915

The men had done the best they could to salvage as much as possible once the shifting subsided. They were remaining on the ship for now for safety and also because most of dog town had been destroyed, but the dogs had become used to having freedom and open spaces. Now that they were back together on a single deck of the ship, it felt worse than when they'd been in the kennels.

Bummer was still refusing to speak to Samson, no matter how many times he'd tried to apologize. Sally said to give him time and space, but that was easier said than done when they were in such close quarters, and Samson missed his friend desperately. The guilt of leaving his friend behind wrenched at his gut. Samson wished there were something he could say, something he could do to make it right again, but in the end the fact remained that he'd abandoned Bummer when his friend had needed him the most, and Amundsen had turned out to be the better dog after all.

Samson wandered across the deck to see if the boss was busy. Shackleton sat at the very front of the ship—a lone watchman, monitoring the ice for any sudden changes in the floe. Samson went to join him, drawn both by the need for companionship and the mouthwatering smell wafting from a tin can in the boss's hand.

Shackleton started slightly as Samson approached from behind, then gestured for the dog to join him. Samson lay at his feet, and Shackleton patted his head gently as the two of them looked out at the icebergs surrounding them. Samson glanced up at whatever the boss was eating. It smelled delicious. He couldn't help but move closer to sniff at the tin.

"You hungry, boy?" The boss smiled.

Samson gave a gruff bark, and Shackleton chuckled. "Well, I don't much like sardines anyway, so you might as well have the rest," he said, placing the tin on the ground in front of Samson.

Samson plunged his face into the tin, chomping away at the smoky fish and licking every last corner, making sure he hadn't missed a drop of juice. Satisfied, he lay down, licking his chops.

The boss stood up, shielding his eyes as he gazed at the sun. "Eventually there will be more ocean than ice," he told Samson. "I just hope the ship stays firm until then and we make it home."

Samson looked up at the boss, surprised. Shackleton had always seemed so sure, so in control of everything, even when things were going wrong.

"I'm glad I have you to confide in," Shackleton said. "I can't tell the crew my fears. We need to keep their spirits up." He smiled. "You must do the same with your team. We must do everything we can to make sure that even if the ship falls apart, we stay strong."

Samson barked and the boss laughed, heading below-decks. "That's the spirit!"

Samson perked up a bit at this. *Finally*, something was happening again. Over the last few months it had felt almost as if they were frozen in time, held within the ice, unable to move forward or back. At least now there was hope again of the ship escaping from its icy shackles.

"So," a low voice purred from atop a stack of crates beside Samson, and he saw Mrs. Chippy peering into the empty tin at his feet. "You're back, are you?"

Samson sniffed, keeping his distance. He didn't much trust cats and still couldn't quite understand why Bummer had taken such a liking to the creature that he'd felt obliged to save her when she'd stupidly thrown herself overboard.

"For now," Samson replied.

Mrs. Chippy licked at her paws. "Shame," she said. "Not that I'm not happy to see you again, I suppose. But I had become used to having the run of the ship. Now it's overcrowded with all these savage beasts taking up the best napping spots."

"Hey!" Samson cried. "We're not savage beasts!"

Mrs. Chippy shrugged. "Maybe not all of you, but I saw what happened during your little race. That dog..." She lowered her voice and glanced around, making sure no other dogs were in earshot. "*Amundsen* knew he would flip the sled and take out at least one of his team with it. Any sled dog worth his salt would have known to slow down at that turn."

Samson gazed at the floor, feeling a hot flush of guilt all over again.

"But..." she purred. "At least he stopped to help poor Bummer out."

Samson let out a low growl. He felt bad enough about it all as it was, without a cat making him feel worse— although he suspected she knew this and was trying to stir up more trouble. Cats were like that.

"How long do you think it will be before we start moving again?" Samson asked, eager to change the subject.

Mrs. Chippy licked at her tail and sighed. "I'm not sure we *will* be moving again."

"What do you mean?" Samson asked, feeling his stomach drop. "The boss said once the ice melts..."

"Take a look around," Mrs. Chippy told him. "The ice is pressing *against* the ship."

Samson peered over the side of the ship. The cat was right. Large folds of ice reached up against the hull, higher than ever. There were areas where chunks had broken up, but instead of falling away, new waves of ice had pushed up and over the old to replace them.

"What does that mean?" Samson asked, although he already knew the answer.

"We're not going anywhere," Mrs. Chippy said, slinking away with her tail held high.

Samson sat in stony silence for a while. *The boss is a clever human*, he thought. *He'll figure a way out of this. Maybe if I help* . . . He jumped up and ran down the gangplank onto the floe before anyone could stop him, scratching and scraping desperately at the ice against the hull to clear it, but it was useless. His claws barely scraped the surface. The ship was stuck tight.

A couple of weeks passed with no sign of the ice easing up. If anything, it seemed to be getting worse. At night Samson could hear the creaks and groans of the ship, almost as though it were in pain from being so constricted by the ice, the life being slowly crushed out of it. There was a definite tilt to the ship now. Samson's kennel on one side of the deck was at least a foot higher than the kennels opposite. Most of the crates and anything else that might pose a hazard had been secured by ropes, but occasionally something would slide down the deck, pursued by dogs as though it were a game and not a terrible warning of what might be to come.

The boss had ordered the men to prepare supplies in

case they needed to make an emergency evacuation, and the entire crew, including Shackleton, had been taking shifts throughout the day, hacking away at the ice in the hope that it might give the ailing ship a bit of space to breathe and settle once more. But their efforts turned out to be useless. For every chunk of ice the men managed to break free with their axes and picks, more ice would quickly move up to replace it.

That night, Samson found it hard to sleep. The moans of the ship seemed even louder than usual. He closed his eyes again, trying to dream of happier times when he could run on the ice, when he felt a sudden shudder beneath him.

"Bummer!" Samson called, forgetting their feud. He dug his claws into the wooden deck as the ship jolted again. "Something's happening."

Bummer scowled, but then his eyes widened as there was another jerk. Just as the boss ran out onto the deck, the *Endurance* vibrated, shaking loose supplies and sending anything that wasn't secured crashing down onto the deck. Kennels, dogs, and equipment flew across the deck in a jumble of ropes, wood, and fur. Then, just as quickly as it had started, everything went quiet. The dogs and men held their breath as one as the vibrations stopped—and then all at once, the ship jumped clean into the air, landing on the ice with an almighty crash to settle on solid ground. The entire ship now leaned to the port side, its hull and beam exposed.

"Are you all right?" Samson asked Bummer as soon as he remembered to breathe again.

Bummer just stared at Samson, his eyes huge and his body trembling. Samson thought he must look the same way. Although the vibrations had stopped, his legs shook and his heart hammered.

"The ship jumped out of the water," Bummer said, his voice trembling. "The pressure must have been so great that it squeezed it right up and out of the water. Pop!"

"At least it didn't crush it," Samson said, relieved they were all still in one piece.

"No," Bummer said slowly. "But how are we going to sail to land when the ship is no longer in the water?"

CHAPTER 12
BUMMER

October 27, 1915

A heavy fog lay over the ship. Not the usual weather-type fog that dissipated with the sun, but the heavy weight of doom and gloom that seemed to have settled on them, harder to ignore with each day that passed.

What will we do now? It was all Bummer could think about. With the ship veering to one side and not even resting in the water, how could they possibly move anywhere? They couldn't take the lifeboats and sail to safety—they were still surrounded by thick pack ice for hundreds of miles in every direction. Even with the sun warming the ice, the temperatures were low enough that it might never thaw completely, or even enough for new leads of water to open up and guide them to safety.

Bummer felt on tenterhooks every time he felt the slightest judder or movement or heard the smallest of creaks from the ship. It seemed as though the *Endurance* itself were made of ice and could shatter to pieces around them at any moment.

There was a yell below, and McNish hurried up onto the deck. "We've got a leak!"

Several men joined him as they raced down into the bowels of the ship with Mrs. Chippy swiftly running past in the opposite direction.

"There's water everywhere," she moaned, her fur sodden and her tail dragging along miserably behind her. "On the starboard side. It looks as though the planks gave way."

"Will the ship sink?" Bummer asked.

"I hope not," Mrs. Chippy replied. "I do hate getting wet."

Bummer could do nothing but wait while the men worked the pumps below for three days and nights, until the water was gone and there was no more danger of sinking. The boss and the captain walked around the ship, inspecting the damage to the rudder and hull.

"I wish we could do something to help," Bummer told Sally. "I feel so useless."

"I'm not sure there is anything we can do," she said, swatting at the pups, who were climbing over her back.

"What will we do if the ship is lost?" Nell asked, her blue eyes wide.

"We'll carry on just the same on the ice," Sally reassured her. "We are ice dogs, after all. It is where we belong."

"I'd rather live and die somewhere a bit more comfortable," Bummer grumbled. "By a warm fire, with a big, juicy bone to chew on and not an icicle in sight."

"But then we'll never get to meet Father," Nell sniffed.

"This is an adventure," Sally told Nell, drawing the pups close. "One day you'll be able to tell your own pups about the amazing journey you made and, I hope, your father, too."

They listened as the ship groaned and creaked. The timbers gaped and twisted as though the ship were alive, taking deep breaths, in, then out again as the crew and dogs willed it to hold on.

The boss returned, and an eerie silence fell on them. Even the ship was quiet for once as they waited for what Bummer hoped would be some good news.

"We are to abandon ship," the boss said, his head hung low. "It is no longer safe to stay here, and the ship is irreparably damaged."

That was it, then? They were doomed to live on an ice floe forever.

There was a murmuring of voices; then the men got to work. They began unloading stores, equipment, and crates from the ship to set up camp on the ice now that it had settled. The dogs and men were uneasy about going out there again, but they had no choice. The ship was no longer safe. The men lowered three of the lifeboats filled with supplies to the ground. Out on the ice, the sleds were piled up with as much as they could comfortably take and the dogs could pull.

Bummer was following the other dogs toward the gangplank when a shadow fell over him. Mrs. Chippy was stretched out precariously on the mast above, her tail flicking gently back and forth as she surveyed the scene.

"Are you coming?" Bummer asked.

She shook her head. "I am the ship's cat," she said. "I'll remain with the ship for as long as I can. Then I might do a little exploring—I'm sure I can do a much better job than the men and dogs have managed." She glanced at Bummer. "No offense. Who knows, I might even be the first cat to make it to the South Pole."

Bummer watched Samson ushering the pups down the gangplank while Roger tried to ride on his tail.

"Maybe...maybe I could come with you?"

Mrs. Chippy gave him a kind smile. "Cats are solitary creatures, Bummer. Besides," she said, gesturing to Samson, Sally, and the pups, "you belong with them."

She turned to slink across the narrow wooden beam, putting one paw carefully but purposefully in front of the other.

"He left me behind," Bummer said quietly.

"Maybe so," she said. "But out here on the ocean, fortunes can change in an instant."

"Technically, we're not on the ocean," Bummer started, but Mrs. Chippy had gone. A set of small footprints in the snow was the only sign she'd been there at all.

On the ice, the men set up tents and unloaded supplies. The dogs returned to what remained of their old dogloos, hoping they would be rebuilt. Bummer felt sorry for the humans. Despite their thick clothes and heavy fur gloves and hats, many shivered as they worked, their faces as white as the snow around them. A group gathered around the captain and Bummer wandered over to see what was going on.

"They don't have enough fur sleeping bags for each human," Sally told him as they watched the men choose and pull a piece of string from the captain's enclosed hand. "They have to draw lots."

"They'll freeze out here," Bummer said. "Humans have the thinnest skin I've ever seen."

"Maybe we can help?" Samson suggested, coming to join them. He gave Bummer a small smile.

Bummer thought for a moment about what Mrs. Chippy had said, giving a small smile in return. "How?"

"Our fur is thick—maybe we can sleep alongside the men to keep them warm?"

"Nice idea," Bummer said with a small laugh, "but I'm not sure they'll want a beast like you in a tent with them. There's barely enough room for the humans, let alone a dog twice their size!"

"It was a nice idea," Sally said, smiling at them both.

"The boss is making a speech!" Nelson said, running over to their mother.

"Ship and stores are gone," the boss told the group solemnly. He took a deep breath. "So now we go home."

"So that's that, then?" Bummer asked. "The expedition is over. We are going home."

He sat for a moment, letting it all sink in.

But it wasn't as simple as all that, he thought, as the realization of the terrible situation they were in fully dawned on him. They were stranded on an ice floe drifting farther away from land every day. Nobody from the outside world knew where they were, or even that they were still alive.

"The goal now isn't simply to get home," Bummer whispered. "But to survive."

CHAPTER 13
SAMSON

November 1915

Dog town was miserable. It wasn't the grand place it had been when the dogs were free to run and play. Now there was the constant threat of the pack ice moving, and of being crushed by rising walls of ice or being pulled down into the depths of the ocean as the floes ripped apart. It was impossible to sleep.

The men no longer took the dogs out on long trips with the sleds for fear that the landscape would change too quickly. Their magnificent ship, which had been built to last and endure, was slowly being defeated, day by day. Every day it seemed to list even more as though giving up the fight. The masts cracked and broke apart and the hull was crushed as the ice pushed and pulled the ship this way and that.

They were now hundreds of miles from land. The closest was somewhere to the west. Now that the ship was beyond salvation, Samson wondered how they were ever to reach land. What would happen as the ice floe began to break up and flood? They couldn't live on the barren ice raft forever. Their daily servings of pemmican were already being rationed, so that now they only had two meals a day.

Sally and the pups bounded over to Samson's dogloo.

"We're on the move!" Roger said excitedly.

"On the move to where?" Samson asked, trying not to bang his head on the ceiling as he stood to see what was going on.

"Home!" Nell said.

Sally shook her head slightly. "Home is a very long way away," she told Nell. "We're going to march across the ice to reach land."

The men were taking down their tents and loading supplies into the three lifeboats, while close by some of the dogs were being put into their harnesses.

"We can't pull those boats!" Samson choked. "A

sled is one thing, but a boat that size, filled with provisions..."

"We're not pulling them alone," Sally said, trying to smile for the sake of the pups, although she clearly felt as anxious as Samson. "We're going to work as one big team with the men."

The thought of actually doing something, *going* somewhere, was appealing to Samson. He'd had enough of sitting around and waiting. At least there was a plan, a goal to work toward rather than simply waiting on the ice.

But even with the men helping to pull the lifeboats, Samson knew it wasn't going to be easy. The landscape was filled with obstacles: walls of ice, thin ice, snow several feet deep in some places, not to mention the shifting floes. He couldn't help feeling a terrible sense of dread. As much as he trusted that the boss knew what he was doing, things felt wrong. Every sense in Samson's body tingled with nervous apprehension.

When he led his sled team, Samson knew the best routes to take and what to avoid. It was relatively easy to maneuver out of danger with a team of dogs on his side. But that kind of teamwork had taken months to build up. There would be no quick turns or going back to safety with the lifeboats and gear in tow. If they were confronted with trouble, there was very little chance of getting out of it.

Samson joined his and Amundsen's teams as they were leashed to the same lifeboat. Amundsen's eyes looked duller than usual, and he seemed thinner. They all did, Samson remembered, since their food had been rationed—especially the men, many of whom hadn't had much meat on them to begin with.

Once they were harnessed—dogs and men both, the men having tied ropes around their waists that were attached to the lifeboats—they set off: a parade of men, dogs, and boats marching across the hostile terrain. Samson strained, digging his claws into the ice for a better grip as they puffed and heaved and pulled, the lifeboat behind them feeling as heavy as though they were pulling the *Endurance* itself.

"This is impossible," Sally groaned behind him as the puppies ran alongside. "It will take a lifetime to get anywhere at this pace."

Samson agreed, but he didn't have the energy or breath to say so out loud. As long as the men kept going, he would keep going, too. The boss hadn't given up yet, and neither would he. They pulled on into the night, resting only for a few hours before continuing beneath the moonlit sky. Some of the dogs struggled more than others, and each day when they put their harnesses back on, Samson noticed that there were fewer dogs. He glanced back at Bummer every few hours to see how he was coping. To his surprise, Bummer seemed to be doing as well as any of the others, including Hercules and Wolf. Amundsen did not look as well. He wheezed in and out as he struggled against his harness.

Behind him, Bummer stumbled, jolting the main harness.

"Keep up!" Amundsen growled between wheezes. "All of you. You're stronger than you think. Let's show the boss what we're made of."

Bummer straightened at the back, looking as surprised as Samson at Amundsen's outburst, but it seemed to have done the trick. The dogs began moving more steadily together, as a team, even though some of them had never worked together before.

After three days and nights, despite their best efforts, the *Endurance* was still in plain sight behind them. They had barely made any progress, and many of the dogs had fallen ill...or worse. Some had collapsed out of pure exhaustion, others from lack of food, water, and rest.

"This isn't working, is it, boy?" Shackleton said to Samson while the others slept. "We'll run out of food before we ever reach land."

Samson licked the boss's face in sympathy. Shackleton scratched behind Samson's ears in return. Samson wished he could tell the boss it would be all right...that the men and dogs had faith in him. But instead he lay on the boss's feet to warm them, the only way he could think of to make him feel a little better.

The next morning, the boss ordered the men to set up Ocean Camp. Tents were erected for the men and new dogloos built for the dogs. That night, Samson had the best sleep he'd had in his whole life, and the next morning he awoke feeling strangely stronger than ever. He joined a new sled team made up of the stronger dogs, and Wild took them back to the *Endurance*, where they salvaged everything and anything they might use from the ship to set up their new camp: sleds, food, fuel, and whatever equipment they could find. They pulled everything back to Ocean Camp on the sled. After a short break, they set off again, picking at the remains of the once-magnificent ship until there was little left.

As they hauled the final load back to their camp and rejoined their friends, Samson turned around to look at the *Endurance* one last time. Time seemed to slow down as parts of the ship broke off, crashing onto the ice. Bit by bit, the ship was squeezed and crushed and devoured by its foe.

"She's going, boys!" the boss called out as men and dogs watched what was once their home slowly disappear, piece by piece, into the Weddell Sea, until there was nothing left but debris. They stood in silence. Even though they had been expecting it, no one had the words to express the devastating loss of the one thing tethering them to the hope that they would survive: That they would one day return home.

Samson lifted his head to the sky and howled a lament for the fallen ship. The puppies followed suit. Slowly every voice joined theirs, the men's included, as their howls were carried on the wind. A farewell to the only home the pups had ever known, and any chance of honor and recognition gone with it.

CHAPTER 14
SAMSON

December 1915

It seemed to Samson as though their ice camp were a boat adrift on the ocean with no oars or engine or sails. They were at the mercy of the ocean currents, carrying them out into the unknown.

"Maybe we will eventually drift back to land?" Sally said as she and Samson sat in the glowing warmth of the blubber stove.

"Do you think that's possible?" Samson asked.

Sally shrugged. "Some of the men seem to think so. Perhaps we could at least get close enough to make an escape attempt on the lifeboats."

"Or maybe we'll float back toward the Antarctic to continue our adventure?" Samson said, half joking.

He knew that even if they could reach Antarctica now, they'd have no chance of making it across the continent. Even with the supplies that the Ross sea party had laid out, they had too few provisions to make it to the first post. The Ross party had set out from the Ross Sea on the opposite side of Antarctica, making their way along previously used polar routes to lay out supplies for when Shackleton reached the Beardmore Glacier. But that was so far out of reach now, and many of the dogs were sick from worms or exhaustion. Every time they went out on the sleds, there seemed to be fewer and fewer of them.

At least his friends were well, Samson thought. He couldn't bear it if anything happened to them. They were as close to Samson as family. He just wished Bummer would forgive him.

"Have you seen Amundsen lately?" Samson said in a low voice.

Sally nodded. "I think he's ill...not that he would admit it. Too pigheaded to know when he needs help and too proud to ask for it. He's been giving his food away to the pups, says he's not hungry, but there's more to it than that."

Samson lifted his head toward the tents, from which the sound of the banjo and the men singing jolly tunes floated on the wind. "What do you suppose they have to celebrate?" he asked.

"Something called Christmas," Sally said. "Surly told me. He said they've finished off all the good food, without giving us a sniff."

"I'd give anything to taste something other than pemmican or seal blubber," Samson sighed, laying his head on his paws and letting his eyes drift closed to dream of lamb chops and gravy.

The next day, Samson was awoken by a flurry of activity in the camp. The men had taken down their tents and were loading the lifeboats back up with everything and anything in sight.

"We're on the move again," Sally told him with a sigh.

Samson groaned. "Not with the lifeboats?"

She nodded solemnly.

"It was hard enough when we were healthy. Now..." He gestured around at the dogs gathering. Their numbers were dwindling day by day. Samson could count at least twenty dogs missing—Amundsen included. He couldn't bring himself to ask Sally if Amundsen was still sleeping or sick ... or worse.

"Mother says we're going on another adventure!" Roger said, rushing up to greet them, his tail wagging excitedly. He gripped Samson's tail in his jaws and Samson spun, swinging Roger around and around until he felt dizzy.

"Me next!" Toby yelled.

Samson laughed and shook his head, trying to stop the ground from swaying beneath him.

"We might be big enough to help pull the boats," Nelson added.

"Do you think they're strong enough?" Samson asked Sally, flicking his tail back and forth to stop Toby from hanging on.

Sally glanced at the playful pups, who didn't seem to have a care in the world. "I'm not sure I'll have much say in the matter," she replied. "We're short of dogs, and all of us are weaker—the men included."

She gasped at something behind him. Samson turned to see what had caught her attention. Making his way through the crowd of dogs was Amundsen. He had lost more weight, and tufts of his fur hung in patches.

"He's not thinking of pulling the boats?" Samson said, unable to take his eyes off the dog who had once been so strong. Samson had always considered Amundsen invincible—as tough on the inside as he was on the outside. But now he seemed broken.

"What are you all staring at?" Amundsen snarled. "We've got a job to do—I suggest we get on and do it. Wolf, Hercules, are you coming?"

The dogs remained silent. Wolf and Hercules kept their eyes on the ground, neither able to look at Amundsen.

Amundsen caught Samson watching. Samson held his gaze for a moment before nodding. "You heard what Amundsen said. Let's get harnessed up."

Amundsen gave Samson the slightest of nods, then shuffled over to Crean.

The march was slow and exhausting, pushing many of the men and dogs almost to the breaking point, but they had to reach land one way or another. There was no other option. Once the weather warmed, there would no longer be a solid ice floe beneath them. Samson kept an eye on Amundsen, and eventually they were moving so slowly that Crean shifted Bummer and Samson forward to help Amundsen lead the pack. Samson couldn't help smiling as Bummer gave Crean a huge grin, his eyes filled with pride and determination.

Beside him, Amundsen coughed and wheezed as he huffed in and out.

"Amundsen," Samson started.

"Don't worry about me," Amundsen snarled. "Worry about your own team! Surly's barely breathing back there."

Samson caught Bummer's eye as he moved forward to stand side by side with Amundsen, pulling at the ropes. Bummer did the same, moving to Amundsen's other side so the three were level, keeping pace with Amundsen to ease his burden a little without it looking as if he was struggling. Amundsen opened his mouth to say something but then closed it, giving a small nod.

The days passed and their pace grew slower and slower as they headed across the floe toward the pale blue line of open water far in the distance. There didn't seem to be any one dog leading the pack anymore. As exhaustion overcame even the strongest of dogs, they all hung in a group, cheering one another on when one or more fell behind, with barely more than a huff. They had to stop often to allow the weakest dogs at the back to catch up and rest for a few minutes before being urged on by the men, who were just as exhausted.

A few days later, some of the men had decided they had had enough.

"I'm not going any farther," McNish declared, dropping the ropes and collapsing onto the ground. "We'll all be dead before we get anywhere near the water."

Some of the other men agreed and joined McNish on the ground. The dogs, grateful for even the shortest of breaks, took the opportunity to collapse on the ice, many of them falling asleep within minutes.

The men gathered around, having a heated discussion with the boss as to what they were doing and who was in charge. In the end they seemed to come to some kind of agreement, and Wild returned with a face like thunder. "The boss won't forget this, McNish," he growled as he began removing the dogs' harnesses. "Neither will I."

"We're setting up a new camp, boys," Wild told the dogs. "Welcome to Patience Camp."

Samson glanced over at Bummer. He lay on the floor, and his chest heaved up and down as he breathed. Samson thought of Amundsen and how much he was struggling. He couldn't stand it if something happened to his best friend, too. He drew up his courage and the last bit of strength he had left in his legs and limped over on sore paws to talk to Bummer.

"Bummer," Samson said, taking a deep breath and hoping his friend wouldn't reject him once more. "You were right. We are a team, and I let you down. I let my pride get in the way of what was most important, and I'm so, so sorry." He nudged Bummer's head gently with his, and Bummer smiled.

"I forgive you," Bummer said. "I won't say I'll forget about what happened, because I can't, but...with things the way they are, we need to stay strong. For Sally and the pups and for all of us to make it. We're stronger together than apart."

Samson felt a rush of relief. "We are," he said.

Bummer nodded, then gave a shy smile that reminded Samson of the first time they'd spoken.

"Seven days," Samson puffed. "Seven days we've been pulling these lifeboats across the floe, and now we're just giving up?"

"We don't have much choice," Bummer replied, unable to stand. "Open water could be hundreds of miles away, maybe more. We've only covered half a mile a day, if that. It would take us more than a lifetime."

Samson knew Bummer was right. Samson was one of the strongest dogs, and even he felt he would have been unable to go much farther, but giving up meant hope was lost. At least while they were moving...while they were doing *something* to reach salvation, there was still hope. Now that hope was slipping out of their grasp. How long would it be, he wondered, before there was none left at all?

CHAPTER 15

BUMMER

February 1916

Rations were running low. As the weeks in Patience Camp melted into months, dogs and men seemed unsure whether they were ever going to leave or whether they would stay until there was nothing left to survive on and the ice swallowed them up. To Bummer's dismay, Amundsen remained leader of their sled team, each hunting trip more arduous than the last. But at least Amundsen didn't seem to have gotten any sicker, and they were all noticeably thinner and weaker now. The lack of three full meals a day was taking its toll on their bodies and minds.

They headed out with Crean, searching for anything

they might be able to add to their paltry diet. Until recently, they had been finding plentiful wildlife—seals, penguins, and fish—swimming deep below the ice shelf. As time went on, it seemed as though their prey had either decided to move on, or that there were simply none left.

They had been out on the floe every day that week, but to no avail. It had been weeks since they'd had anything other than their single daily portion of pemmican, and the men were no better off than the dogs. Who knew how much longer it would be until there was nothing left?

Bummer watched Amundsen at the front. Amundsen winced as he moved. He was as stubborn as a mule and refused to show the slightest weakness, even if it was clear to them all that he was in pain. Amundsen gritted his teeth, as though trying to bite back the discomfort that was obviously building inside him. Bummer couldn't understand why Crean couldn't see it. Amundsen shouldn't be out pulling the sled at all, let alone leading the team. It would put them all at risk if anything happened to him.

"We should take a different route," Bummer called

out as they set off, knowing that Amundsen would likely ignore him. They had taken the same trail for the last three days and come up empty-handed. Bummer was sure Amundsen had chosen the same path across the floe because it was flatter and slightly easier to navigate. But that also meant that any potential prey could spot them coming from a mile off and would be long gone by the time they reached it.

As expected, Amundsen ignored him, pulling to the left along the same old path.

"There's nothing out this way," Bummer insisted. "We need to take a different route."

Amundsen glanced back at Bummer, his eyes flashing in warning, and kept going.

"The lad's right!" Judge shouted. "Let's try a different route."

Amundsen snarled, continuing to pull the sled to the left. Bummer caught Judge's eye as he began resisting the command, leaning instead to the right toward a less-traveled route. Judge veered the same way, the weight of the two of them having an effect on the others. Then, to Bummer's surprise, Wolf and Hercules joined them, the entire team pulling away from their leader.

"We need to find food, Amundsen!" Wolf growled apologetically.

Amundsen's pace slowed. He no longer had the strength or authority to force his team his way, so he joined the others, staring back at Bummer before changing direction.

Bummer knew he would likely pay for his insubordination later, but they needed food. He could probably go on for a while on their meager rations, but the pups couldn't. Bummer was determined not to return to camp until he had something to bring back to them.

As the hours drew on, the hope Bummer had of returning to camp victorious faded. They'd seen no other signs of life all day. Bummer worried that if they continued like this for much longer, the dogs might start turning on one another—or at least the younger and weaker dogs. When the hunger became too much, who knew to what lengths the others would go to stay alive?

"There's nothing out here," Amundsen snapped. "I hope your little coup was worth it?"

"At least we tried," Bummer said firmly.

They turned back toward camp, heading wide around a fissure of broken ice, a slash of dark water like a gash in the landscape. Bummer hesitated as they neared. He thought he saw a flash of something silver beneath the water. They drew closer, the dogs ahead of him passing the opening one by one. As if out of nowhere, a leopard seal emerged from the water, launching itself into the air, its mouth open wide, revealing rows of razor-sharp teeth, and aiming straight for Crean. Bummer spun as fast as he could, angling his body backward to catch the seal by the neck. He held on tight.

The seal was almost twice his size and twice as strong. It rolled over, forcing Bummer beneath it, crushing his legs, but Bummer still held on, refusing to let their one chance of a good meal escape them. The dogs slid to a halt, joining Bummer with excited barks to help him pin the leopard seal down. Wolf and Hercules took the seal's tail and dragged it off Bummer, while Judge and Amundsen circled, blocking any way the seal might have of escaping into the water.

Crean leaped off the back of the sled, yelling, "Hold him! Hold him down, boys." His feet slipped and slid over the ice in his haste to reach them and suddenly went from under him. Crean flew up, landing on his back with a hard thud and a loud groan. He carefully got back onto his feet and finished the seal off with a single shot from his gun. The sound echoed around the ice, stunning them into silence.

"It could have killed you," Wolf said, his eyes wide, looking between Bummer and the leopard seal. "It's bigger than me."

"Looks like we'll have something to bring home after all," Judge said, giving Bummer a wink. "That was some quick thinking there, lad."

"You did good," Amundsen grunted, then returned to the sled.

Bummer couldn't speak. Shock and adrenaline pounded through him as what he'd just done slowly sank in. It had been pure, raw instinct. Almost as if he'd known what was about to happen a split second before it did so that he was in the right place at the right time. Crean patted Bummer on the head, then loaded the seal onto the sled.

When they reached camp, Crean hauled the seal over to the makeshift galley. McNish had built it using the remains of the ship's wheelhouse, complete with a stove built by Hurley, fueled with blubber. Much to Bummer's embarrassment, the dogs crowded around as Wolf,

Hercules, and Judge recounted the tale of how Bummer had not only found food but had also saved Crean from the attacking seal.

"It was nothing," Bummer mumbled, not used to the attention. "I did what any other dog would have done."

"Oh, I don't know about that." Samson grinned. "I told you he was a good hunter," he announced loudly to the other dogs. "Didn't I tell you?"

A rush of warmth ran through Bummer as the dogs asked questions about how he'd held on and when he'd first noticed the seal. Sally smiled at him proudly and Bummer grinned so much his jaws hurt. He'd never done anything so heroic before; it had taken him by surprise even more than the others. He basked in the glory, his tail wagging until it hurt. The best part of it was that they would all get to eat something that wasn't pemmican.

There was a yell from the men crowding around the galley to take a look at their catch, and the dogs ran over.

"Look at this!" Crean shouted. "We're going to have a feast tonight, boys!"

Bummer stepped forward to see a huge pile of fish on the ground beside the leopard seal.

"The seal must have caught those fish just before you nabbed him," Samson said, licking his chops at the sight of all that fresh food. "Don't forget some for Bummer," Samson barked at the men, even though he knew they couldn't understand him. The other dogs joined in, barking Bummer's name at the men until they seemed to get the message, and in that moment Bummer realized what it meant to belong, to be part of something that would last for a lifetime, no matter the outcome of the expedition.

"There's enough for everyone!" Wild told the dogs, laughing.

The men handed out portions to the dogs, and Bummer headed back to his dogloo, his jaws clamped around two large silverfish. Amundsen was curled up in his dogloo, not even attempting to get some fish for himself.

Bummer dropped his fish at the entrance. "You should get over there before the fish is all gone," he said. "Wolf and Hercules have already gone back for seconds."

Amundsen grunted, then shuffled around awkwardly so that his back was to Bummer.

Bummer looked down at the fish, then over to the galley where the last of the men and dogs had drifted away to eat their meals.

"To be honest," Bummer said, "I don't really like fish that much. They disagree with me, if you know what I mean."

Amundsen remained silent, but his ears had pricked up slightly.

"I'll just leave these here," Bummer said. "In case anyone else wants them. It would be a shame for them to go to waste." He paused for a moment, then headed off toward his own dogloo.

"Wait!" Amundsen snarled behind him.

Bummer turned, and Amundsen looked down at the ground, then back up at Bummer. "Thank you," he said, gingerly picking one of the fish apart with his teeth and claws, swallowing down the smallest of pieces.

"You should see Dr. Macklin," Bummer said quietly.

Amundsen sighed. "There's no point."

"What is wrong, Amundsen?"

"My stomach," Amundsen said, wincing again as he tried to swallow some more fish. "I think it's worms."

"We'll get you some help," Bummer said finally. "You can have half of my food rations every day, and I'll see if I can get Crean over here to look at you."

Amundsen gave him a grim smile. "I think it's probably too late."

CHAPTER 16

SAMSON

March 1916

Samson could feel the swell of the ocean beneath the floe as he tried to sleep. It had been building day upon day. First, there had been nothing more than the smallest of vibrations beneath the ice, like the tickle of a slight breeze on his fur. But then the tremors had built so that at times, it felt as if the entire earth were shaking and the ground could collapse at any moment. Samson would have worried less if there had been some kind of backup plan, or if they had still had the *Endurance* to flee to when the ice did eventually break up. But now they had nothing but three lifeboats filled with provisions and barely enough room for the men, let alone the remaining dogs.

In some patches, the ice had become so thin that Samson could see the occasional sea creature or fish gliding along in the ocean beneath the shelf—close enough to spot its fins and tail as it passed, but not close enough to be able to reach out and grab it in his jaws.

There was a yell outside his dogloo, and Samson ran to see what was happening. A large crack had torn right down the center of camp, with the men and dogs stranded on one side and the lifeboats on the other, slowly drifting away.

"We have to get to the lifeboats!" Bummer said, running over to Samson with a wild, panicked look in his eyes. "They're our only hope. If we lose the boats, all is lost. *We* are *lost!*"

"Calm down," Samson said. "They aren't going very far."

The floe had only moved a few feet before stopping again, having been enclosed by more ice. The boss and some of the men leaped over the gaping crack and heaved the lifeboats back to their bigger floe.

"We can't stay here much longer," Bummer said gravely. "More ice will break away until there's nothing but ocean."

Samson knew Bummer was right—they all did. He was sure the boss had a plan; he always did.

"The boss won't let his crew perish," he told Bummer. "He'll find a way."

Sally came over with the puppies hot on her heels. Samson couldn't believe how much they'd grown; they were already almost up to his chest—and he was a big dog.

"We're leaving," she said, puffing to catch her breath. "The boss just announced it."

"See," Samson said to Bummer. "The boss has a plan."

"The men are sorting through the provisions now," Sally continued. "We're going to take what we need and no more. The ice has broken up enough for us to reach open water."

"But where will we go?" Samson asked, looking out over the vast nothingness in all directions, a sense of unease twisting in his gut. "If the *Endurance* couldn't make it to land, how are the lifeboats supposed to?"

"The boss said we've shifted enough that we can reach land," Sally said. She looked at her puppies chasing each other on the ice. "I didn't think my pups would ever get to see it," she whispered.

"Bummer!" Wolf called out, racing over the ice toward them. "Come quick!"

"Amundsen?" Samson asked as Bummer raced off after Wolf.

Samson and Sally followed the dogs to Amundsen's dogloo, where Hercules, Wolf, and a few others crowded around.

"What is it?" Samson asked Bummer.

Bummer shook his head slowly. "He's not doing well, Samson."

Sally stepped forward. "Can I speak with him?" she whispered.

Samson gestured to the other dogs to move back.

After a few moments, Sally returned, her eyes filled with tears. "I've said my goodbyes," she sniffed. "Maybe you should, too."

Samson followed Bummer into the dogloo, his heart and mind racing as he thought of what he might find inside. "What can we do to help?" Samson asked quietly.

Amundsen raised his head slightly off the ground and gave a weak smile, then shook his head. "Just... could you stay with me?" he asked.

Bummer nodded, and he and Samson settled down beside Amundsen.

They sat in silence, listening to the hustle and bustle outside as men and dogs prepared to leave. Samson wondered whether they should tell Amundsen what was going on—but what would be the point? he thought sadly. Amundsen hadn't been a friend of his, but he had a deep respect for the dog—his strength, his speed, his leadership. Bummer had told Samson how Amundsen had saved him from beneath the sled, and Sally had told him how Amundsen had shared his food with the pups.

"Amundsen," Samson started. "I'm sorry I didn't invite you to race."

Amundsen was quiet for a moment; then he gave a small, gruff laugh. "You were afraid I'd beat you."

He was still again; then he raised his head to look at the two friends sitting beside him and sighed. "I wanted to be alpha so badly. I thought making friends would make me appear weaker. Bummer...I was glad to have you on my team. I'm sorry you got hurt because of my own pigheadedness."

Bummer shook his head, his eyes glistening. "You remind me a lot of my brother," he said. "He was the one who was chosen to come to England, but our master didn't want to let him go, so he sent me—a poor replacement. I didn't think I would ever find somewhere I belonged. But I learned, and I changed, and I think you did, too, Amundsen. When it mattered the most, you put yourself aside to help others. No dog left behind, remember?"

"You earned your place out here," Amundsen said. "I wish..." He paused to catch his breath, wheezing as he breathed slowly in and out. "I wish we could have been friends."

He coughed once more, then laid his head back on his paws.

Samson listened to his breaths as they slowed, getting quieter and quieter until he realized he could hear them no longer.

"We were friends, Amundsen," Bummer said quietly. "We were friends."

That night, the dogs gathered around as Crean dug a grave deep in the snow for their comrade Amundsen. Every single dog was there, wanting to pay their respects. When they were in trouble, when Sally needed him or when Bummer was hurt—Amundsen had never let them down. He had been there for them, and they were now here for him.

Finally, Crean drove his shovel deep into the ice, then returned to camp, his head low, leaving the dogs alone.

"Bummer," Samson said after a while, breaking the silence. "Do you want to say something?"

Bummer moved to the front of the crowd to face the remaining dogs. They had lost so many over the last few months, so many dogs who had succumbed to the harsh Antarctic conditions, one by one. It seemed as if hardly any of them were left.

Bummer opened his mouth to speak, but no words came out. Instead, he threw his head back to the sky and howled. Samson, Sally, Hercules, Wolf, and all the dogs did the same, howling a final farewell to the strongest and boldest of them all.

Amundsen.

CHAPTER 17
BUMMER

April 1916

The boss had been right about them drifting back where they'd come from. For the first time they could see an outline of land in the distance—barely a dark blot on the horizon, but there nevertheless. *Elephant Island.* Finally, they had a destination, something to head toward and focus on rather than simply drifting like the floe themselves, through the endless days of hunting and sleeping and waiting.

The others were almost as excited as they'd been when they'd first set out all those months ago. Bummer couldn't help but get swept up in their renewed enthusiasm and energy. The men had reorganized their supplies—food rations, fresh water in barrels, small stoves on which to heat their food, along with anything else essential to the long journey ahead. Only two reduced sled teams remained now, along with Sally's pups, who were still too small to pull the sleds. The dogs were divided among the three lifeboats—the *James Caird*, the *Dudley Docker*, and the *Stancomb Wills*.

Bummer was disappointed to find he'd been allocated to the *Stancomb Wills* along with Judge, Hercules, and Wolf, while Samson, Sally, and her pups were on the *James Caird* with Shackleton.

"We'll be back together soon enough when we reach Elephant Island," Samson reassured him.

"However long that will be," Bummer muttered. His stomach lurched at the thought of being back on the water, but he wasn't filled with fear as he had been when they'd first set out on the *Endurance*. Since then he had been through worse things than a little bit of seasickness. He would survive this just as he had survived the trip all those months ago.

Although he'd rather have been with his friends, Wolf and Hercules had been kinder since Amundsen died;

Bummer knew he was just as good as they were, and he didn't care what the others thought any longer.

"It will be over before you know it," Samson said. "Try not to think of how you feel while you're on the boat, but rather how you will feel when you get off it and step onto solid land."

It was good advice, Bummer thought, but he had little control over his stomach. There was also the matter of the pack ice that lay ahead. Once in the boats, they would have to find their way through the maze of water passages until they found one that would lead them out onto the open ocean.

"Are you ready to go?" Sally asked, coming over to say her farewells to Bummer and Judge.

"As ready as I'll ever be," Bummer said, licking the pups on the head in turn to say goodbye.

"We'll miss you," Nelson said as they headed to their boat.

"You'll see me again soon," Bummer reassured him.

Samson turned to follow Sally, but Bummer called him back.

"Samson," he started, searching for the right words to say to the best friend he'd ever had. A way to say goodbye if they didn't make it to Elephant Island. Bummer knew their chances were slim, but at least there was a chance.

"Good luck," he said finally.

Samson smiled and nudged his head against Bummer's. "You too," he said.

Bummer laughed and gave Samson a small nudge in return; then Samson was gone, directing the other dogs to their boats and giving words of encouragement to those like Bummer who didn't relish the idea of going out onto the water.

Bummer headed over to the *Stancomb Wills* and jumped on board, joining the dogs in the middle of the boat and trying to take up as little room as possible so that the men could do what they needed to do to keep the boat afloat. He found himself wedged between a large crate filled with something sweet-smelling and a rolled-up canvas, which he laid his head on, closing his eyes so he didn't have to see what surrounded them.

He didn't need to see in order to feel, though. As they floated on through the leads, the water became choppier, the boat rising up and over each oncoming wave. The waves seemed to be pushing them back toward the ice, telling them it was a bad idea to even attempt to cross the sea. But the men were determined, and so they resisted, even when the waves grew higher, crashing onto the deck and soaking men and dogs until they were so wet and cold that they might as well have just swum.

Another large wave crashed over them. The men bailed out water with whatever they could lay their hands on, but the raging sea wasn't their only obstacle. They were still surrounded by pack ice and floes, the smaller pieces smashed up by the churning ocean as they were pulled this way and that. The chunks of ice broke off, floating atop the waves. Each time the sea rose to assault the boat, it threw blocks of ice at them, some as big as Bummer's head, as though they were under attack from the sea itself, threatening to capsize the boats before they had barely started.

"How are you holding up, lad?" Judge asked, ducking to avoid being beheaded by another missile of ice.

Bummer could only groan in response, glad for once that he didn't have a bellyful of food, as it wouldn't have lasted long.

"Chin up," Judge said. "I have a feeling it's going to get a lot worse before it gets better."

They continued on—day after day without any release or respite from the assault of the wild sea. Bummer's eyes felt swollen and sore, stinging from the salt constantly being thrown in his face along with the icy water. His mouth was the only part of him that was dry, since he'd had only the smallest sips of water from the barrel when the men had time to stop wrestling with the ocean. His fur was matted. In the rare patches where it wasn't soaked through, the salt had dried, coating it with a thin layer of white powder that he was unable to clean off.

Bummer had never felt so miserable in his entire life. Part of him wished they would be capsized just so that the ordeal would be over. But that would mean he'd never see Samson and Sally again, and the thought of his friends helped him to endure. He thought of Amundsen and how he would act if he were on the boat with them. He wouldn't moan or groan or feel sorry for himself, no matter how cold or hungry or wet he was. Bummer made a promise that he would try to be more like Amundsen.

A greater threat than thirst and hunger lurked nearby, however, getting ever closer. For the past few days they had been followed by killer whales. At first the whales kept their distance, the sound of air being blown out through their blowholes the only clue that the gigantic mammals were there at all. But as they sailed on, the whales seemed to get more curious, moving closer to the boats, their tall, curled fins rising out of the water, until the men became afraid that they might attack and drag the boats down into the depths below.

That night, Bummer looked out over the edge of the boat as the dark shapes rose out of the water, only yards away. Their strange song echoed all around. Bummer barked to get the men's attention, but no one came. The men were either too tired or too focused on getting to land.

A large black-and-white head emerged from the water, two big black eyes staring right at Bummer as he tried to catch his breath.

"H-hello there," Bummer said to the whale.

The whale watched him for a while, then opened its gigantic jaws to reveal a set of sharp teeth. Bummer backed away from the edge of the boat, but the whale didn't attack. The sides of its mouth pulled up into a smile.

Bummer stepped forward on shaky legs and gave a little smile back.

"Would it be possible for you and your friends to keep your distance?" Bummer asked, figuring he had nothing to lose. "It's not that we aren't happy to see you, but we're afraid you might sink our small boat. We're trying to get to Elephant Island," he explained.

The whale seemed to laugh at this, letting out a series of clicking sounds.

"I know it seems like an impossible mission." Bummer sighed. "But we've been lost for so long, and we're trying to find our way home."

The whale considered this for a moment, then disappeared silently beneath the water. Bummer watched and waited to see if the whale would return, then was startled by the sound of more whales breaching the surface. The whale appeared again behind them. The boat suddenly jolted as the whale pushed the boat forward, steering them off to the left while its friends did the same with the other lifeboats.

The men started to yell, at first out of pure terror at seeing the gigantic beasts at the stern, but then in amazement as it became clear that the whales were trying to help them. After only a few minutes, they'd traveled almost as far as they had all day. The whales disappeared again, gliding away from the boats.

A large head appeared once more, turning to look back at Bummer.

"Thank you!" Bummer barked.

The whale let out a high-pitched cry, then was gone, its huge fin rising out of the water as it dived beneath the waves to follow its pod.

CHAPTER 18
SAMSON

April 1916

After four days at sea with little to eat and drink and even less sleep, the boats passed alongside an ice floe big enough that the boss decided they should camp off the boats for the night. Samson finally understood how Bummer felt when he got seasick. The moment he set foot on the solid ice, the world around him spun. His legs wobbled as he tried to adjust to stillness rather than being thrown perpetually back and forth, up and down. He slowly lay down and closed his eyes for a moment, waiting for his brain to catch up with his body and stop swaying from side to side.

"You look as bad as I feel," a voice said with a laugh.

Samson opened one eye and grinned at Bummer, glad to see that his friend was well.

"You don't look so bad," Samson said, his tail wagging as he slowly...very slowly...sat up. "In fact," he said, "you look positively well compared to the rest of us."

"I just kept in mind what you told me," Bummer said. "And focused on being back on solid land rather than on the boat."

"And that worked?" Samson asked, surprised. He'd only told Bummer that to make him feel better, but if it had worked for Bummer—the most seasick dog he'd ever known—then maybe he'd try it when they were back on the boat.

Samson groaned out loud at the thought of having to go back out on the relentless ocean. "Do you think we could just stay here instead?" he asked Bummer, looking around at the ice floe. It wasn't very big—Samson could see its edges—but it wasn't moving. Maybe he should just stay there? Live out the rest of his life on the floe, catching fish for food and building an igloo for shelter.

"But what about the *honor*," Bummer teased, "and the *recognition*? You'd get none of that if you gave up now. No one would even remember your name five years from now."

Samson frowned. "I'd hope that you would," he said indignantly.

Bummer grinned at him and Samson sighed. Bummer was right. He could no more stay here when they were so close to reaching land than the boss could. He would keep going for as long as he was able and for as long as it took until they were safe.

The men had tethered the boats securely to the floe and set up tents on top of the ice. Sally and the pups were curled up together fast asleep, and soon Samson and Bummer were the only ones still awake, the rest of the expedition having given in to their exhaustion.

"I'm going to try to get some much-needed rest," Bummer said with a yawn. "Are you coming?"

Samson shook his head. "In a while. I want to make the most of being able to stretch my legs."

He trotted off in the opposite direction, lurching sideways a few times as his body adjusted to the solid ground. His legs soon caught up and he raced across the ice, howling as the air filled his lungs and he felt freer than he had in a long time. He stopped to catch his breath and gazed around him. The Weddell Sea was treacherous, but the landscape was beautiful. Samson had never really stopped to look—*really* look—at the beauty that surrounded them. All around, icebergs rose up out of the water, twisted and molded into a myriad of shapes like sculptures created by nature itself. The ice sparkled as though it were coated with stardust, and Samson doubted that anyone had ever seen anything like it.

He trotted toward the tents, weariness finally getting the better of him, and headed over to where the dogs lay together in a cozy huddle. As he settled down beside Bummer, there was a terrible cracking sound. Samson whirled around, searching for the source of the noise. A fissure snaked through the ice, weaving this way and that, sneaking closer and closer to one of the tents at the edge of the camp. As it moved, it grew, splitting the floe apart to reveal the black water beneath.

Samson barked as loudly as he could as the fissure disappeared beneath the tent. There was a loud splash and a yell as one of the men inside fell into the glacial water below. Samson tore his way into the tent, searching the water desperately for the man. He caught sight of a patch of dark fabric and grabbed it in his jaws, pulling as hard as he could. The man Samson recognized as able seaman Holness emerged, thrashing about in the water, gasping air. Samson realized that he was trapped inside his fur sleeping bag, which was dragging him down. Samson held on as tight as he could, unable to move any farther. The weight of Holness and his sodden sleeping bag was just too much, even for him. But he wouldn't let go. No matter what happened, he would not lose one of the men now.

Other men and dogs arrived, and together they hauled the shaking, shivering man from the water, pulling him far away from the fissure to safety and wrapping him with their own sleeping bags as the color slowly returned to his cheeks. He nodded at Samson in thanks as he drank some cocoa warmed by the tiny stove.

"Well done, old boy!" Shackleton said, ruffling Samson's fur. "That was some quick thinking."

Samson beamed up at the boss with pride.

"Time to move on!" Shackleton shouted. "It's not safe on the floe."

"You heard the boss!" Samson barked as men and dogs reluctantly made their way back into the boats.

Honor and recognition, he repeated to himself as he stepped back on board. *Honor and recognition.*

The men took turns rowing while the others tried their best to stay warm. Samson felt more helpless than ever. On land he could do *something*, be useful in *some* way, but out on the open water, there was little he could do but feel sympathy for the men as they strained against the oars, and lie on their feet to help warm them as water and ice lashed at their faces. The temperatures were so low that each time the men swapped places, their thick gloves had to be chipped away from the wooden oars.

Instead, Samson focused on the dogs with him in the boat, making sure that the pups were as warm and as dry as they could be, and that the weaker dogs were eating and drinking what they could, when they could.

The boats were tethered together as Bummer's boat—the *Stancomb Wills*—was having trouble keeping up, seeming to be the least sturdy. Whenever Samson glanced Bummer's way, the men on the boat seemed to be constantly bailing out water. He hoped Bummer was all right. They were surely going to reach land soon?

The men called out to one another to change shifts, but Captain Worsley remained frozen in place. Samson watched as the men lifted him from the bench in a sitting position, his arms and legs rigid. Samson made room as the men laid him on the bottom of the boat, gently easing his legs down until the blood began flowing through them enough that the poor fellow could move again.

The boss decided they all needed a short break, so he boiled up some water on the stove and handed out their daily rations—one biscuit. It was all they could spare. Without a proper stove to mix up the pemmican for the dogs, there was little alternative. Samson took a small nibble at the edge of his biscuit, trying to make it last as long as possible. Then he saw Nelson gazing at him, a forlorn look on his face. Nelson was by far the biggest pup and had already gobbled his biscuit down in one gulp.

"Do you want some of mine?" Samson asked.

Nelson nodded. "I'm so hungry," he said. "My stomach won't stop growling."

Samson bit off a piece for himself, then slid the other half to Nelson, despite the protests from his own growling stomach.

"We'll reach land soon enough," Samson said. "Then there will be plenty of food. I'm sure of it."

The wind picked up, and Shackleton called out for the men to continue onward as a blizzard swept in. Soon the boat and everyone in it were covered in a blanket of white. Half the men on board rowed, trying to find their way through the swirling blizzard engulfing them, while the other half bailed out water. But it seemed that for every bucket of water they threw out, two bucketsful were thrown back in from the sea. The men were fighting an impossible, never-ending battle as they blindly continued on, while Samson could do little more than watch and hope.

CHAPTER 19
BUMMER

April 16, 1916

Bummer was so exhausted, hungry, and thirsty when they finally reached Elephant Island that at first he thought he must be hallucinating.

Seven days.

It had taken them seven grueling days, traveling over the most treacherous of seas, fighting against everything nature had to throw at them—waves several feet high, blocks of ice being hurled at them from all directions, the constant threat of being sunk, gales, blizzards. They had made it through it all and had come out the other side alive. Very much the worse for wear, but alive.

At times, when it had all become too much to bear

on the boat and Bummer had felt he might lose his mind, he had heard a small voice in his head, a presence beside him that seemed to be urging him to hold on. He didn't know where it had come from, but he clung to it with all his might, repeating over and over in his head: *just a little farther, just a little farther.*

And now here they were. Elephant Island wasn't what Bummer had been expecting, although after being away from land for so long he only had hazy memories of what land was supposed to look like. He had been expecting more color, though. After spending months surrounded by nothing but dazzling white or complete darkness, he had been looking forward to seeing something...else. But Elephant Island was small, barren, and gray, looking both uninviting and inhospitable. The island was surrounded by threatening, craggy cliffs. The beach they landed on was barely more than a sliver. It was coated with rock and stone and shingle that made it impossible to move faster than a slight trot as the grit stuck uncomfortably between Bummer's toes.

The men quickly set up the tents and stove as far away from the shore as they could, and Bummer hurried over to the sweet scent of pemmican being prepared.

A few weeks ago he would have given anything to eat something other than the dried meat concoction, but now it smelled as heavenly as a roasted turkey. Bummer impatiently waited his turn, sniffing at the other dogs' meals as they dug in, his mouth watering so much that he had to lap at the drool pooling at the edges of his jaws. Eventually, he got his meal. He began gulping it down, even though it was too hot and burned his tongue. Then he slowed, taking his time to savor each mouthful as though it were the last meal he would ever have. Finally, satisfied, he joined the other dogs and fell into a deep slumber, feeling more content than he had in a very long time.

April 17, 1916

Bummer's excitement was short-lived. Their small beach was unsheltered from the elements, and the wind and rain raged at them. Numerous times, the men had to chase after tents and supplies that had been blown out into the small bay. To Bummer's horror, Shackleton suggested that they return to the boats to sail to a more hospitable part of the island. Bummer would have preferred to stay where he was, but as a blizzard began to draw in, he knew they would have little chance if they did that.

They navigated the boats carefully around a peninsula to the west, where they set up Wild Camp. Bummer thought it certainly lived up to its name. They were no better sheltered than where they had come from, but there was more space, and plenty of seals and fish.

No sooner had they arrived than a gale blew up around them. There was no time to erect tents or build any kind of shelter, so the men dragged the boats up onto the shore and turned them over, creating temporary shelters. Men and dogs huddled together miserably beneath the boats, listening to the wailing storm outside and the crash of waves on the beach.

"This is almost as bad as being out on the boats," Bummer muttered to Samson, who was huddled against him.

"I thought there would at least be more...*land*," Samson replied. "So that we could run and race... maybe even make a home here."

Bummer peered out at the raging storm beneath a gap at the bottom of the boat.

"We can't stay here," he said, his gut twisting. "We're not made for this type of environment."

Bummer felt Samson nod beside him, but he stayed silent. Both knew that they had sailed for salvation only to find themselves just as stranded. Bummer didn't know what the boss's plan was, but it needed to be a good one, because Elephant Island was not a place where men or dogs could survive for very long.

CHAPTER 20
BUMMER

April 20, 1916

It had quickly become clear to Bummer that they couldn't just sit on Elephant Island and wait to be rescued. No one in the outside world knew they were there, and they were not on any shipping route, so there would be no passing ships, whalers, or fishermen to hail. The only chance of rescue they had lay with them alone, and what limited resources they had left.

Bummer sat at Wild's feet as he chatted with Captain Worsley, hoping to scavenge a few scraps of food from them when Shackleton joined them. The boss bent to ruffle the fur on Bummer's head and broke off a piece of the dry biscuit he had in his hand, passing it to Bummer.

"We can't stay here," Wild told Shackleton.

The boss nodded, then smiled. "I know. That's why I have come up with a plan!"

Bummer's ears pricked up, eager to find out what the boss had in mind, and Shackleton winked at him.

"We are going to sail back to South Georgia," Shackleton declared.

Wild spat out the water he had been drinking. "We...How are we going to do that? The men barely made it here in one piece."

"McNish can fix up the best boat, make her as seaworthy as possible, and then I'll lead a group of us back to Grytviken, where we can get help. I'll need you, of course, Worsley, and perhaps McNish to keep him out of trouble. We can decide the others later."

Shackleton looked at the two men staring at him openmouthed. "Come on! We've got work to do."

The three men set off. The boss paused. "You too, Bummer. We need every man and dog to help out."

Bummer scrambled to his feet, caught up in the boss's excitement. It was exhilarating and terrifying at the same time.

The boss ordered McNish to set to work on the most

stable of the lifeboats—the *James Caird*. Bummer kept the carpenter company as he worked, remembering Mrs. Chippy. After the ship was lost, Bummer had returned to search for her, but there had been no sign of the sly cat apart from a few small footprints leading away from the shipwreck to disappear into the snow.

"What's he doing?" Samson asked, joining Bummer on the rough shingle beach.

"He's making her seaworthy," Bummer replied, watching as the carpenter worked quickly with his tools to rebuild the hull, strengthening it with wood from the other boats and using the mast from the *Dudley Docker* to reinforce it.

"Isn't she already seaworthy?" Samson asked. "She made it all this way over here, didn't she?"

"Yes," Bummer said slowly, unsure whether to tell his friend what he had overheard or keep it to himself for now. He knew that as soon as Samson found out about Shackleton's crazy endeavor to head to South Georgia, he would want to go along. Selfishly, Bummer wanted Samson to stay on the island. It was going to be hard enough being left behind on Elephant Island without his best friend being gone, too.

In the end, Bummer realized he had no choice. Samson would go whether Bummer wanted him to or not, and he couldn't persuade him otherwise.

"The boss plans to sail to South Georgia," Bummer said finally. "To Grytviken whaling station."

Samson barked with laughter; then his jaw dropped when he saw Bummer's serious expression. "But that must be hundreds of miles away! He plans to sail all the way? In that small boat?"

Bummer nodded. "The captain reckons it is at least seven hundred miles away, maybe more."

Samson blew out a long puff of air as he shook his head slowly.

They sat in silence for a while, watching McNish work feverishly. He fitted a canvas sheet over the top of the boat, securing it tightly with nails to provide waterproof shelter for the men to escape to. Samson and Bummer tried to be as helpful as they could, bringing him pieces of wood and tools and other things they thought he might need, but after Bummer dropped a hammer on his foot, McNish chased them away.

Other men brought sacks filled with heavy stones and sand to create ballast for the hull of the ship, to make it more stable and ensure that it wouldn't easily capsize when confronted with the huge waves they were likely to be up against out in the open ocean. Melted ice was poured into kegs and placed in the hull along with food and provisions.

"How long do you think it will take to sail all that way?" Samson asked.

"There's enough food to last for four weeks," Bummer said, the enormity of the task Shackleton and his men were about to undertake weighing heavily in the pit of his stomach. "If they haven't made it to South Georgia by then, all hope will be lost."

April 24, 1916

"I'm going to go with the boss," Samson announced. "I need to see this expedition through to the end."

Bummer didn't bother to argue. The boss had already chosen his crew of men—McNish, Worsley, Crean, and able seamen Vincent and McCarthy, and, of course, Shackleton himself. There was only one obvious choice as to which dog should accompany them. As second-in-command, Wild would be in charge of the men and dogs staying behind.

"Don't leave, Samson!" Roger cried as the men and dogs gathered on the beach to say their farewells. "Who will teach us how to pull a sled properly?"

Sally laughed. "I don't think any dog could pull a sled over these rocks."

"You have Bummer here to teach you everything you need to know. He will be taking my place as leader while I am away," Samson said, winking at Bummer.

"I didn't know any dog had appointed *you* leader," Bummer retorted, but he supposed that since Amundsen had died, it had been more or less accepted by the dogs—even Wolf and Hercules—that Samson was their unofficial leader.

"You'd better tell Judge that." Nelson frowned. "He's been bossing me around all day."

"Will you come back?" Nell snuffled. "So that we can get home to our father?"

Samson paused. Bummer knew he couldn't make such a promise. "He will try his very best," Bummer said as Samson nodded at him gratefully.

Samson said goodbye to each of the pups in turn,

touching his nose to theirs. Then he rubbed his head against Sally's.

"We'll see you again," Sally said sternly. "This isn't goodbye, just farewell for now."

The boss whistled to Samson.

Finally, Samson turned to Bummer. "I will miss you, old friend," he said.

Bummer swallowed, trying to find the right words. "I'll miss you, too," he said. "Make sure you return to us."

Samson took a deep breath, then bounded across the beach and into the *Dudley Docker*, which carried them to the *James Caird*, moored a little way out in the bay.

As they sailed away, Samson turned and barked over the cheers of the men: "Honor and recognition!"

Bummer ran into the water until only his head and shoulders remained above. "Honor and recognition!" he barked back, watching until the boat was a small blot on the horizon.

"So now we wait," Bummer whispered to himself, looking out over the water as it sparkled with reflected sunlight. At least they had chosen a good day—the sea was calmer than Bummer had ever seen it, and it had been the first time since they'd arrived on the island that the clouds had faded long enough for the sun to appear.

Bummer hoped that was a good omen and the weather would last. Samson had a long journey ahead of him, and he would need all the luck he could get if they were to make it to South Georgia.

CHAPTER 21
SAMSON

Late April 1916

The *James Caird* navigated out of the small bay, heading for open water. Samson took a moment to take in every detail of Elephant Island: the dark, craggy rocks and tall cliffs surrounding it, the seals basking on the shore close by, staying just out of the dogs' reach. In the distance, snow-topped mountains glittered in the sunlight like tall beacons. Samson hoped he would see those beacons again when they returned for their friends, guiding them in the right direction.

The sea had been relatively calm at first, but as they sailed away from land, the choppy waters hit, slapping against the hull of the boat to splash frigid water in Samson's face. Samson knew he'd have no chance of sleeping even if he wanted to, although the carpenter had done a pretty good job on what the boss jokingly referred to as *belowdecks*. The canvas sheet at least provided enough cover so that the men and Samson could take turns beneath it to eat some food and get what little sleep they could.

They carefully navigated through the narrow passages, between the pack ice and past vast icebergs that rose to the sky, just as they'd done on the *Endurance* all those months ago. The boat was already being jostled this way and that. Once they were out in open water, there would be nothing to soften the blows.

As night fell, Samson and three of the men, Vincent, McCarthy, and McNish, retired below to prepare some food on the small stove, making something they called hoosh. Samson's mouth watered as his rump pressed tightly against the water kegs while the men sat cramped together with their knees up to their chests, huddling around the dull warmth of the stove. Vincent mixed beef, a chunk of lard, oatmeal, sugar, and salt with water from one of the kegs. The concoction made a kind of stew that was rather like pemmican but had a strange aftertaste. It was better than blubber, though, and Samson lapped his portion up gratefully.

Once they had finished, they lay down as best they could, soaking, cold, and shivering as they tried to get some rest, turning out the dim light from a small oil lamp hanging above their heads. Samson tossed and turned, trying to find a comfortable position, but every time he did so, he ended up sticking a paw or tail in one of the men's faces, much to their annoyance, so he decided to keep the boss company above decks.

The sky was filled with clouds that only drifted away for the briefest of moments to reveal the stars by which Worsley tried to navigate. Worsley stood shakily, holding up a peculiar metal instrument, while Crean and Shackleton clung tightly to his legs to steady him. Samson watched curiously as Worsley lined up the instrument with a small patch of stars in the sky. But no sooner had he started than the sky clouded over once more, so that Worsley was only able to make an educated guess as to whether or not they were heading in the right direction.

Worsley turned with a sigh and, seeing Samson back on deck, decided to go down below for some food. Samson made his way over the top of the canvas, being careful not to step in the wrong place or lose his footing and be thrown overboard. He sat beside Shackleton at the bow as they gazed out into the nothingness surrounding them. Without maps to guide the way, Worsley navigated by estimating their direction and the distance they had traveled. Samson had no idea how this worked, but the boss seemed to have faith in Worsley, so Samson decided he should, too.

May 2, 1916

The men were sick, and Samson wasn't in much better condition. But at least his fur coat kept him warm, even if it was sodden. The men's own coats were soaked through, and they were freezing. Two of them had frostbitten ears and were barely able to hold down anything the boss gave them to eat or drink. Samson remained above the canvas. At first he had tried to lie with the men to warm their bodies with his own thick fur. But as the stench of illness grew stronger, it became too much for Samson to bear.

They had been sailing for ten days and nights.

Worsley had estimated that they were halfway into their journey, although with the limited readings he was able to take, it was hard to tell. For all Samson knew, they could be heading in the opposite direction, or going around in circles. There was nothing but the rare glimpses of the sun and stars in the cloudy sky to help Samson get his bearings.

The boss ordered the others to get a hot drink inside them, worried that they would all catch the sickness until there was nobody left but Samson to steer the boat. Samson remained up top, keeping watch. He turned to look behind them and spotted what appeared to be a thin line of clear sky not too far in the distance. Samson barked to get the attention of Shackleton, who in turn called down to Worsley to bring up his instrument to take a reading. It had been days since the sky had been clear enough to do so. One wrong calculation and they could end up hundreds of miles off course.

Samson kept his eye on the thin line. It seemed to be moving, not in the gentle way that clouds move, but in a way that made Samson realize that he wasn't looking at the sky at all. He jumped up, barking a warning to the men, trying to urge Shackleton and Worsley belowdecks as the line galloped closer. It was not a clearing in the sky at all but a colossal wave thundering toward them like a herd of angry elephants, set to destroy everything in its path.

Samson barely had time to dive beneath the canvas before the thundering wave hit. The roar was deafening. Samson braced himself, waiting for the water to rush in as the boat was knocked sideways by the immense force. But miraculously, the boat remained afloat. Samson released a deep puff of air as he realized that the only reason they hadn't capsized was likely the handiwork of McNish, with a whole lot of luck thrown in for good measure.

The men quickly bailed out the water that filled both the hull below and the deck above. Some of the food rations and water in the kegs had been spoiled, and anything that had been slightly dry was now as waterlogged as Samson's fur.

"Most of our water has been tainted by seawater," McNish said. "We've probably one day's worth of drinking water left...if that."

"We'll have to ration what there is," Worsley said.

McNish grunted. "Our rations were small enough as it was."

Samson watched helplessly as they continued to bail out water for almost an hour, keeping watch for anything that might pose a threat or be useful to the boss—especially any more mammoth waves. When the men had done all they could, they joined Samson above decks, sitting in a shivery silence, knowing that none of them would have any chance of sleeping after such a close brush with disaster.

The following day, they had the first glimpse of real sunlight since they had departed from Elephant Island. It felt to Samson like more than a lifetime ago, and he couldn't quite remember why he'd been so keen to go along with Shackleton rather than remain on the relative safety of solid ground that wasn't constantly trying to drown him or toss him back and forth.

Worsley stood on the canvas at the bow, as steady as he was able. Shackleton and McCarthy held on to his legs and he held up his instrument to the sun, finally able to get a more accurate reading. Samson feared the worst: that they had drifted in the wrong direction and would be even farther from their destination than when they'd started—although he thought maybe that wouldn't be so bad if they were heading toward Canada so that he could just return home. He shook his head at himself for his selfishness. The pups were counting on him—they all were.

"We're still on course," Worsley announced, to Samson's surprise. "If nothing terrible intervenes in the meantime, we'll reach land in a few more days."

Samson felt his stomach and muscles unclench for the first time since he'd set foot on the *James Caird*. They were almost there. They were going to make it.

CHAPTER 22
SAMSON

May 7, 1916

Samson lay on the canvas deck, gazing out at the water, searching for any sign of land. He'd finally found his sea legs again, and the constant swaying up and down, to and fro, no longer bothered him. He hadn't yet spotted anything that looked even remotely like land, apart from the time he'd mistaken a floating patch of brown seaweed for a rock.

As they continued on, more patches of seaweed bobbed alongside the boat like watery companions, and it occurred to Samson that the only other place he had seen seaweed before was on the shore at Elephant Island. He jumped up and barked excitedly.

"What is it, boy?" the boss asked, just as a pair of huge white birds with yellow beaks and the largest wings Samson had ever seen circled overhead, calling out to the boat below to see if they had any fish to offer.

Albatrosses.

The men laughed at the sight, clapping each other on the back and shaking hands, while Samson joined in, wagging his tail and jumping up at them until they included him in their celebration. If there were birds, there was land close by. But their jubilation was short-lived. Dark clouds drew in, bringing with them gale-force winds that threw up the sea around them, jostling the small boat as they tried to hold course, fighting against the elements with every last bit of strength they had left.

That night was one of the worst Samson had ever spent on the boat. Through the constant rain that bombarded them, they could finally see the dark outline of land in the distance. South Georgia. They headed closer to the bay, across the choppy water, but the high waves threw them this way and that, and as they drew nearer, they found themselves surrounded by sharp rocks, jutting threateningly out of the water.

"It's too dangerous!" Worsley shouted above the screaming noise of the gale hurtling around them.

Samson dug his claws into the boat as they were smashed up against the side of a large rock. It scraped painfully along the side of the boat as the men tried to navigate around it without causing any damage.

"We have to go back out into safer water," Shackleton ordered.

Samson felt his nerves loosen a little. As much as he wanted to be back on solid ground, the risk of trying to make it to the bay was too high.

With the gale making it impossible to steer the boat safely, they were forced to wait for the storm to die down. They had finally reached land after fourteen days at sea, but they couldn't get to it.

After a few hours, the boss decided to attempt the hazardous landing once more. They were all exhausted, hungry, and dehydrated. Their energy was draining by the minute as their effort to stay afloat and not be drawn farther away by the surging sea took its toll. Samson hadn't drunk any water for a couple of days because their water supply had been tainted when the large wave had attacked. In his exhausted, dehydrated state, the bay looked to Samson like the open jaws of a wild wolf, with jagged teeth surrounding them on all sides, preparing to gobble them down whole.

The wind seemed to have died down a little, and the way ahead was clear enough that they could slowly weave around the rocks in the water. Land drew closer, closer, closer, until Samson could see the seafloor beneath them when he looked over the side of the boat. The moment it was shallow enough, he jumped from the boat, leaping and splashing through the water as though his energy had returned to him in one fell swoop. He shook himself and raced off, barking at the men on the shore below when he found a small stream trickling down the rocks nearby. After filling his belly with the cool, fresh water until he was fit to burst, he saw the land as he remembered it all those months ago. Above the rock lay swaths of green hills, covered with wildflowers and tall grass that swayed in the breeze. Samson couldn't remember ever seeing anything so glorious in his life. He longed to run free along the lush green hills forever.

The men unloaded the stores that hadn't been damaged or ruined by the salt water, then crawled to a nearby cave for shelter from the wind. They had no energy to drag the boat onto the shore, so they took turns watching it while the others attempted to get some rest in their wet clothes and sleeping bags.

Samson kept the first man on watch—Worsley—company. Somehow, Samson didn't feel as drained as the men. He felt strangely alive, full of energy that started like a ball of fire in his belly and spread out to his limbs until he could hardly sit still for excitement. They were so close to finding help for their friends. He couldn't understand why the men were all just sitting around when they had such an important mission. Who knew what was happening on Elephant Island while they slept here?

Worsley scanned the bay, then pulled out a smudged piece of paper, its lines and pictures barely legible where the paper had been soaked by seawater. He held up the paper, and Samson saw that it was some kind of map. Worsley traced his finger from one spot, labeled *Haakon Bay*, all the way over a patch of triangular ridges and down to the other side of the island.

"Grytviken," Worsley said with a sigh as he ran his finger back and forth between the two points.

All the energy Samson had suddenly dispersed. Between Haakon Bay and the whaling station lay mile upon mile of mountains and glaciers. They had sailed more than eight hundred miles across the ocean only to land on the wrong side of South Georgia.

CHAPTER 23
SAMSON

May 12, 1916

Haakon Bay was surrounded by steep mountains and glaciers. The bay itself was a small cove, the only shelter being the cave set deep into the base of one of the mountains. Although it wasn't the most comfortable of shelters, Samson thought it was the best place he'd had to lay his head in a long time. He was finally able to dry his damp fur by the warmth of the fire, and eventually he had to move out of the cave because for the first time since he'd been in the kennels in London, he'd felt too hot.

All around the foot of the mountain, plants and flowers grew, breaking through the cracks between rocks and crevices. Water dripped from the glaciers above, freezing again over the mouth of their cave, creating a sparkling entryway. Albatrosses nested on the clumps of grass between rocks, and the younger ones were easy enough to capture.

Yesterday, McCarthy had roasted the birds over the fire, and there had been enough for a bird each. Samson had stripped off every last piece of meat. After dinner, the boss and Worsley had discussed their next move. The *James Caird* had been so battered that it would be unable to make another journey of any length. Their only route to salvation would have to be taken on foot. As the map had shown, they had sailed to the wrong side of the island. They needed to reach the other side, where the humans lived and worked at the whaling station in Stromness.

McNish, Vincent, and McCarthy were still unwell, so to Samson's disappointment, the boss made the decision to stay where they were for a while longer, to rest, eat, and regain their strength. Samson felt raring to go, but he supposed humans were not as hardy as dogs. While the men continued to rest, Samson looked out over the water, wondering how Bummer and Sally and the pups were faring, and hoped they were well.

May 19, 1916

After several days in the cave, and with the men's health improved, McNish fixed up the battered boat as best he could, so that they could sail around the cove to find a better place for the ailing men to shelter while the others went across land for help. McNish warned that the boat wouldn't make it much farther than a few miles before it capsized. As they set out once more, Samson hoped it would be the final time he ever had to set foot in the *James Caird*. He felt a strange sense of pride in the small boat that had managed to take them where they needed to go, but he would be glad to see the back of it.

They sailed a little way around the island, landing in a sandy cove that seemed slightly more hospitable, although there were no caves. The boss named their newest camp Pegotty Camp, and in place of the cave they overturned their boat for shelter. Worsley, Crean, and the boss began making preparations to move on to the final part of their journey.

"We'll have to traverse mountains and glaciers, heading directly as the crow flies across land to Stromness," Worsley said.

Samson thought it was complete madness. Some of the mountains reached so high that when the fog lay low it was impossible to see their peaks. And the glaciers would pose even more of a threat. Samson knew from experience that snow concealed many hidden dangers. One wrong move and you could be lost over the edge of the mountainside, or fall hundreds of feet into a deep ice crevice. And even if you did survive something like that, there would be no chance of rescue.

Samson followed the men as they walked to the foot of the mountain, discussing which would be the best route and what equipment and provisions they might need. Shackleton, ever the planner, decided that they should take as little as possible so as not to weigh themselves down.

They would leave that night, when the moon was high and full and the snow and ice more solid and stable in the falling temperatures. McNish screwed nails from the *James Caird* into the soles of the men's boots for extra grip, although Samson couldn't see how much good that would actually do them. Vincent, McCarthy, and McNish were staying behind. Although they were fitter than they had been when they'd arrived at South

Georgia, they had neither the strength nor the will left to undertake such a perilous task, and the boss knew that taking them along would only impede their own progress. Samson had decided—whether Shackleton liked it or not—that he was going along, too. He had come this far; he wasn't going to stop at the final hurdle, and he knew he would be unable to bear just waiting, not knowing whether rescue was on the way or not. He would go on this final adventure. No matter what happened, he could feel comfort in the fact that he'd never given up, he'd kept on going right until the very end.

McNish accompanied them to the base of the mountain. His breath was labored as he walked, and his steps became slower and slower until he could go no farther. He fell away with a small "Good luck and farewell" to Samson and the men, watching as they headed toward the east coast.

The moonlight reflected off the glaciers, lighting up their route ahead. The boss had brought along few supplies—food and a small stove to melt water, a rope, and an ax. The men's boots were still sodden. Samson could hear the *squelch, squelch, squelch* of their feet inside as they walked, and was glad of his tough paws.

The snow-covered path rose, their pace slowing as the incline grew steeper. It didn't help their progress when they discovered that the snow had melted slightly and instead of treading on tightly packed snow, their paws and feet sank into the slush. It reached halfway up Samson's legs as he struggled on. After a few hours, they paused for some water at the peak of the mountain, looking out over what was ahead. Samson's stomach dropped as he saw what lay between them and Stromness. The landscape held a range of mountains, with steep, craggy rocks and sudden drops, interspersed with flatter land, carpeted with deep ice crevices that seemed to have been carved by giant claws.

The boss signaled for them to move on, and they ascended the next peak, only to find a steep precipice with no way down other than the way they had just come. Exhausted, Samson turned around, leading the men back down the precarious mountain along the safest routes he could find. They walked on and up the next ridge, only to find the same. Again they retraced their steps. Samson became more and more discouraged as they went, wondering if they would ever make it to Stromness or would just be trapped in the endless maze of peaks and crevices and precipices.

As night fell once more, a cold fog rolled in, obscuring what little moonlight there had been, so that they walked blindly, unable to see more than a few feet ahead, knowing that one wrong move meant it would all be over. The boss tied the rope to each of the men and Samson at the rear, so that they wouldn't lose one another and in the hope that if one of them fell, the others would be anchor enough to save him.

When the sun rose the next morning, it brought with it only more despair. The snow continued to melt, reaching almost up to the top of Samson's legs as he struggled through the heavy sludge.

"We need to rest," the boss said, to Samson's relief.

Samson licked his watering jaws as Crean melted snow in a pot over their small stove before mixing up a variety of ingredients that Samson couldn't identify. The men called it hoosh as before, but by the time it was ready, he didn't care what it was called; he just wanted it in his stomach.

As soon as they had eaten, they continued on, determined to reach Stromness before more bad weather set in. Up and down the mountain range they continued, each time confronted by another impassible path. With the dark night drawing in as they reached the summit of yet another peak, the temperatures dropped. They could barely make out what was in front of them, but they couldn't stop for the night. With his thick coat, Samson thought he might be able to survive the freezing temperatures, but the men would have no chance.

He stopped beside the boss, scanning the mountainside for any possible path down. It had become terrifyingly clear that they had only one choice—stay on the mountainside and die, or risk their lives to somehow get to the bottom.

Samson felt numb—both from the freezing temperatures and from the dizzying sight below. The ever-darkening sky and fog obscured whatever lay at the bottom so that he could only see about halfway down. He looked up at the boss, who still seemed to be weighing his options.

"What do you think, old boy?" the boss asked, patting his head. "Can we make it?"

Samson barked his assent. Staying on the mountain would mean certain death. There was only one choice. He trotted over to Crean, who held the rope coiled around one shoulder, and took it in his jaws, pulling it to the ground.

"What are you two up to?" Worsley asked, laughing at Crean, who began a tug-of-war with Samson. Both dog and man refused to let go of their side of the rope.

The boss ended the struggle, taking hold of the rope. Samson immediately let go and barked, and Crean gave in, letting the boss take the coil.

"We're going to have to risk it, boys," the boss said, gesturing to the edge of the mountain. "It's the quickest—and only—way down."

The boss coiled the rope tightly into a pad, creating a makeshift sled.

Samson glanced down again, suddenly losing his nerve. It was a fool's errand; how could they possibly expect to survive? Dogs were supposed to pull sleds, not ride them down a mountainside.

"It doesn't seem too steep," the boss told them. "We can use our feet to steer or slow down if we need to, and Samson can sit between us. The extra weight should make sure that we don't go too fast."

Crean frowned at Samson, and Samson gave a low growl in return. If the boss thought they could make it, then Samson knew he could at least be brave enough to try. He stepped onto the rope sled, shifting his weight into the best position, then sank his claws between the grooves to get the best grip. He didn't want any chance of being flung off halfway down.

"Well," Worsley said with a sigh, "I'll not be shown up by a dog. If Samson thinks we can do it, I do, too."

Samson gave a small *ruff* of a bark at Worsley, who scratched him behind the ear, then settled on the pad, squeezing himself tightly against Samson's back.

Crean sat behind Worsley and the boss took the lead, sitting in front of Samson at the head of their sled. "Ready?"

Samson barked, using his front paws as they shuffled their feet through the snow, drawing the rope sled to the very edge of the slope. With one last heave, the sled moved slowly forward, the front tipping downward as they set off at a terrifying speed, hurtling up and over

ridges and rocks, going so fast that the landscape was a white-and-gray blur as it flew past. Samson shut his eyes tight and clung to the pad for dear life as Crean hugged his back.

Then, as quickly as it had started, it was over. With a great *whump*, they smashed into a bank of soft snow, which exploded in a burst of white, then slowly drifted back down, covering them like snowmen with a large snow dog in the middle. For a moment all was quiet and still. Then the men began to move, standing shakily and brushing the snow out of their eyes. Samson checked that his limbs and tail were intact. His legs were slightly wobbly and his head dizzy as he tried to focus on something that wasn't moving. He shook his fur hard, sending a flurry of snowflakes up in the air, then turned to stare back at the mountainside.

He couldn't quite believe it. The mountainside was littered with large gray boulders, with a steep overhang on the left-hand side. Carved down its center in a deep, meandering line was the track they'd left behind in the snow.

Samson let out a loud bark of a laugh in disbelief, joy coursing through him. The entire expedition had been fraught with impossibilities and danger at almost every turn, yet somehow, despite it all, they were still here. They had made it!

The boss, Crean, and Worsley laughed, shaking their heads with the same disbelief and letting out loud whoops of joy as they hugged each other. Samson joined in the revelry, bounding through the snow in circles and barking so loudly that it echoed around the mountains.

The boss wound the rope up and hauled it over his shoulder; then, after a brief discussion with Worsley as to which direction to continue in, they headed onward, moving closer to the whaling station with every step.

After a few hours, the adrenaline and renewed vigor from the sled ride had drained away. Exhaustion from walking almost nonstop caught up with them. Samson felt his eyes droop and his steps begin to slow. They had been marching for over thirty hours without a break, and though Stromness was only perhaps six hours away, they needed to rest.

They leaned up against an outcrop of rocks that provided a little shelter from the bitter chill of the wind. Worsley fell asleep immediately, his mouth hanging open to let out loud snorts every time he breathed. Crean and the boss quickly followed, huddled against each other for warmth. Samson settled at their feet, trying to help their frostbitten toes thaw a little; then he laid his heavy head on his paws and let his eyes slowly droop. He listened to the men's snores for a while, as their breathing slowed and their breaths became shallower.

It reminded Samson of his last moments with Amundsen, and he opened his eyes again suddenly, jumping up to listen more closely. The men's faces were pale, their lips a dangerous shade of blue. Samson realized that their exhaustion was so great that they might never wake up.

He nudged the boss's shoulder, but Shackleton didn't stir. Samson tried again, but there was still no response. He moved to Crean, taking his boot in his jaws and tugging at his leg as hard as he could, knowing that if he could get a rise out of anyone it would be Crean.

Nothing.

Samson began to panic. What if he was too late? Why had he let them sleep? Why hadn't he urged them on? He barked at them, licking at their faces between his desperate cries.

Wake up wake up wake up!

But no matter what he did, their eyes remained tightly shut.

CHAPTER 24
SAMSON

May 20, 1916

Finally, Worsley stirred. Samson barked loudly, then licked his face once more for good measure to make sure he didn't fall asleep again.

"Gerroff, Samson!" Worsley groaned, running his hands down his face to wipe off the drool.

Samson turned his attention back to the boss, nudging at his shoulder with his head as hard as he could without knocking him over. Worsley finally came to properly and realized what Samson was trying to do. He shook Crean, calling his name while Samson continued to nudge Shackleton, licking at his face as he had done with Worsley. But Shackleton's breathing was ever so shallow. Samson's gut twisted with the thought that he might never wake up. What would they do without the boss? How could they possibly go on without him to guide them?

Samson redoubled his efforts as beside him Worsley finally roused Crean.

"Just let me sleep," Crean groaned.

"Be glad that Samson woke us," Worsley said gravely. He glanced over at Samson. "How's the boss doing, boy?"

Samson barked as Shackleton began to stir. His face was whiter than the snow around them, and his teeth chattered and his hands shook as he slowly took in his surroundings. Worsley heated some lumps of snow over the stove in a small pan and handed it to the boss first to warm him. Once they were all slightly warmer, they stood groggily and gathered their belongings.

"Have to keep going!" Samson barked, even though they couldn't understand him. He nudged them onward despite their protests as they waded slowly through the ever-thickening snow.

A few hours later, Samson saw his first glimpse of

civilization. He barked with joy when he spotted a small wooden hut in the distance, a thin plume of smoke rising from its chimney. Samson led the men up and over large, craggy rocks, navigating around jagged peaks jutting out of the snow while the wild, chill wind stung his eyes and numbed his paws. He paused as he caught the sound of something on the wind. His ears pricked up, and the men stopped to listen, straining to make out the noise within the whirling winds around them. It came again—the distinct sound of a whistle. Samson remembered hearing it once before, when they had sailed from Grytviken. It was the call to the whalers living in the village to come to work.

Samson ran on, with the men struggling to keep up. At the peak of the hill, he could see all the way down into the bay. Far, far below, Samson spied tiny dark figures, as small as bugs, making their way toward the whaling boats docked in the bay.

"Stromness!" the men yelled.

Samson barked, spurring the men on as he bounded alongside a narrow river, but as he ran, he saw that the ground ahead disappeared. He barked to warn the men behind to slow down before they tumbled right over the cliff's edge. The sound of running water echoed below as the river crashed down onto the rocky beach, creating a small waterfall that flowed out to the ocean. Samson ran along the cliff edge. There was no safe way down. No path or slope to slide down, no rocks to climb.

The boss had already come to the same conclusion. He tied one end of the rope to a nearby rock, winding it around three times, then tying a fisherman's knot to make sure it was secure. Then he tied the other end around his waist. He lowered himself backward over the edge of the cliff, holding the rope as tightly as he could, and began walking down horizontally beside the waterfall.

After a few moments, there came a yell from below and the end of the rope was tossed back up to land beside Samson. He took the end in his jaws and held it out to Worsley. Worsley tied it around Samson's belly, a little too tightly, and Samson had to breathe in to ease the squeeze of the rope as it chafed against his skin. He copied Shackleton, inching himself backward until his rear end hung in the air and his back legs scrambled to catch hold of anything beneath him. But he didn't have long legs like the boss and wasn't able to swing his legs any farther to find a foothold, so he closed his eyes and let go.

His stomach plummeted as he dropped a few feet. Crean and Worsley struggled above to hold on to the rope and keep their footing. Loose pebbles and dirt tumbled over the edge, narrowly missing Samson's head as he tried to slow his racing heart and stop flailing his limbs in all directions like a crazed seagull. The men lowered him slowly toward the bottom of the waterfall, where Shackleton waited.

Samson gazed out over the ocean and fleetingly thought this must be how birds felt when they flew, although once he reached the ground he decided that it wasn't an experience he particularly wanted to repeat anytime soon.

Crean came next, swiftly climbing down the waterfall; then Worsley followed. There was no way to retrieve the rope, so they left it hanging. They set off across the beach and into town. They drew a lot of attention as they walked along the cobbled streets, past the small wooden houses and people setting about their daily tasks. At first, Samson thought it must be the sight of such a large dog in their midst—he was sure that after months without a proper bath or good grooming, he looked more like a wild beast than a sled dog. But when the boss stopped to ask a boy where he could find the whaling station manager and the boy yelled in fright, taking off down the street, calling for his mother, Samson realized it was the men's appearance as much as his own.

He vaguely remembered how they had looked when they'd set off—the men clean-shaven, their clothes brand-new and their boots lightly worn. Now they looked like walking skeletons, with their ragged clothes hanging off them and their boots worn to the soles as they shuffled along. They reached the station manager's house, and Shackleton attempted to straighten his clothes and smooth down his hair and beard before knocking.

The door creaked open and a man's face appeared, his eyes wide as he took in the disheveled-looking group.

"C-can I help you?" he stuttered as he stared at the state of them all.

"Don't you recognize me?" Shackleton asked incredulously as the man stepped forward to inspect them more closely. "My name is Shackleton."

Once the manager had realized that it was the great Ernest Shackleton lurking beneath all that grime and hair, he quickly let them in and invited them to stay as long as they wished. The men took hot baths and were given clean clothes, while Samson was hosed down in the yard with frigid water. He grumbled at first at the indignity of not being able to have a warm bath like the men, but as the water washed away layers and layers of thick grime and dirt encrusted in his fur, he felt like a newborn pup again.

Samson barked at the boss when he first emerged from the bathroom, not recognizing his face now that the buildup of life in the wilderness had been removed. The men and Samson ate until their bellies were full, and Worsley immediately set out again on a ship to rescue McNish, Vincent, and McCarthy in Haakon Bay.

But despite having a full stomach and a blanket to lie on beside the hearth, Samson found himself unable to sleep. A terrible gale had blown into the bay, the winds howling around the small village, reminding Samson of all the dogs who hadn't made it. It seemed almost as if they were calling out to him, telling him he shouldn't rest until his friends were safe and well.

Samson tossed and turned. He couldn't shake the thought that had they not taken the risk of sledding down the mountain, they would likely be out in the storm now. When he did find himself dozing off, he would wake suddenly, with no idea where he was, or where Bummer and the pups were. It was only when the boss came downstairs to join him, settling in an armchair by the fire, that Samson was finally able to sleep a little.

Samson knew that the boss had the same thoughts running through his head and was likely making plans for the rest of the crew to join them. The minute the storm died down, the boss would be right back on another ship, heading for Elephant Island, and Samson with him.

CHAPTER 25
BUMMER

June 1916

Time seemed to move more slowly after Samson left. Bummer missed his friend desperately—his constant optimism and high spirits, reassuring Bummer that everything would be all right and that the boss had a plan.

But that had been weeks ago. What if, finally, the boss's luck had run out? What if his plan had failed and they were as lost at sea as Bummer and the men who remained behind on Elephant Island, their hope dripping away slowly like the melting ice until there was nothing left to grasp hold of?

The day after Shackleton and the men had set off

for South Georgia, the bad weather moved in. The dark clouds in the sky above seemed to mirror the dark cloud of despair that hung over the camp. The bay was filled with pack ice, which had closed in on them overnight. Had the *James Caird* left one day later, they'd all have been stuck on the island.

The men had turned over the remaining two lifeboats to create a shelter, as there was otherwise nowhere to hide from the elements. Sally watched from camp while Bummer and the pups helped to gather large rocks and pebbles from the shore. The men used these to build walls on which to rest the shelter so that it wouldn't be flooded by rain or the incoming tide.

The tattered tents were ripped up and nailed around the bottom of the shelter as a kind of buffer to keep the chilly wind at bay, and as soon as the men were more or less satisfied with their efforts, they retired to the shelter to spend the rest of the day in their damp sleeping bags.

Bummer couldn't stand just lying around all day with no purpose, so he wandered down to the shore, hoping that if he waited patiently enough and quietly enough he might catch a fish or two. He watched for a while until he saw a flash of silver move beneath the surface. He crept closer, his jaws poised over the water, moving ever so slowly closer, closer, closer, until...

"Bummer!" Nelson yelled, splashing through the water and scaring the fish away.

Bummer tried to hold in a groan as he turned to smile at the pups—although he couldn't really call them pups any longer; with the exception of Nell, they were all nearly as big as he was.

"Mother said we were to keep you company. We didn't mean to disturb your fishing," Nell said apologetically.

"No matter," Bummer said. "You four can help me. Between us, we'll have a pile of fish in no time."

He demonstrated his fishing technique to the pups, using a stick that was floating on the surface.

"Usually," he said with a frown, "the fish is a lot faster than the stick, so not as easy to catch."

There was a splash nearby as Roger dunked his head into the water suddenly, emerging with a large silver fish flapping about in his jaws.

"Well," Bummer said, feeling slightly put out that he'd been bested by a pup. "Beginner's luck, perhaps."

Nell, Toby, and Nelson copied their brother, standing

with their paws in the freezing water and watching carefully for any fish that dared swim past.

"It might take a while," Bummer told them quietly. "I've been out here for hours and haven't caught a single thing, so don't worry if—"

There was another splash, then another as Nell and Toby dived for the same fish. Nell emerged triumphant, dropping her catch on the shore beside Roger's.

"It's not so hard," she said with a grin.

Bummer decided that perhaps he should just leave the pups to it and watch from the sidelines, since he clearly wasn't cut out for fishing. If Samson had been there, he would likely have had a pile taller than his head by now.

Bummer looked out to sea, hoping to see a black dot on the horizon and his friend returning, but it was as empty as ever. He glanced back over to the pups, who had given up fishing and were splashing one another in the water. Roger had wandered out a little farther, jumping precariously from rock to rock. A little way ahead of him, a dark shadow moved beneath the water.

"Roger!" Bummer shouted, racing along the shore. "Get away from the water!"

Nell, Nelson, and Toby froze at Bummer's tone as he flew past them, cutting his paws on grit and sharp slivers of rock as he ran.

Roger hadn't heard him. He leaned forward, peering over the edge of the jutting rock as the shadow moved closer, closer.

Bummer threw himself into the shallow water, scrabbling up and over the rocks that jutted out, slowing him down. "Roger!" Bummer yelled. "Watch out!"

Roger finally heard him. Time seemed to slow as he turned to ask Bummer what was wrong. Bummer cried out, jumping from rock to rock, desperate to reach Roger in time as the long, dark shape moved alongside the rock Roger was standing on. Without warning, it rose out of the water. A leopard seal. Twice as big as the one Bummer had caught, with twice as many teeth.

Bummer roared and leaped from his rock, pushing Roger out of the way as the leopard seal's huge body connected with his, sending him flying into the water. The back of Bummer's head slammed onto a rock lying beneath the surface. But he had no time to pause or think. He pushed himself up to the surface of the water, then shook his dizzy head and tried to swim back to

Roger's rock. But the leopard seal was much quicker in the water. It bit down hard on Bummer's paw, and Bummer yelped in agony as he felt the bones in his leg crunch.

The leopard seal moved closer, taking its time, knowing that Bummer had no way of escape now that he had been lamed. Bummer looked back at the pups, hoping Roger had made it safely back to shore, then whimpered as the leopard seal moved in for the kill.

There was a sudden bang, and the seal dropped beside Bummer, landing in the water with a loud splash.

"Bummer!" Sally yelled, running over. "Are you all right? Bummer!"

"What happened?" Bummer asked weakly as the men surrounded him, some hauling away the seal, others leaning over to see if Bummer was still alive.

"Dr. Macklin shot it," Sally said, her voice shaking. "If he'd been a second later..."

Bummer felt his eyes close. He was so tired. The energy seemed to be draining out of him. His head felt light, his breathing slowed.

"Stay awake, Bummer," Dr. Macklin said as Bummer felt himself being lifted out of the water by two pairs of rough hands.

"He's not going to make it," another voice said. "He's too badly injured."

"I don't have any other option," Dr. Macklin replied. "We've lost so many. . . . I have to try."

Bummer tried to open his eyes, but they were too heavy. He felt himself drift away as another voice came to him.

"Bummer? It's me, Sally. Stay strong. I'll be right here with you. Hold on, Bummer."

July 1916

Bummer was unable to walk with his heavily bandaged leg. The bite had been deep, and with limited medical supplies, the doctor had been unable to clean the wound properly. To make matters worse, Bummer found himself unable to eat. His stomach constantly churned with hunger, but when he tried to eat even the smallest of meals, it would come straight back up. Sally had taken to sleeping by his side, checking his every twitch to make sure he was all right.

He didn't need to look at the dogs' faces when they

visited to know that he was very, very sick. He just hoped that when his time came, he could be as brave as Amundsen.

The men spent their days improving their shelter. They had placed a homemade blubber stove in the center, which at first had let off toxic fumes. Thick black smoke from the stove coated the men's faces and the dogs' fur with soot. Eventually Kerr, one of the engineers, came up with the ingenious idea of adding a chimney made from an old biscuit tin. The chimney led from the stove up and out through a hole in the ceiling, so that their lungs were no longer filled with the nasty smoke, which Bummer knew was doing him no good at all in his current condition.

As winter drew in, Bummer grew weaker. His only joy came in the evenings when Sally and the pups gathered around him and they listened to the men playing the banjo and singing songs. Often while the dogs slept, Bummer could hear the men talking about their favorite foods and what they would eat when the boss returned and took them home. Most of it, Bummer hadn't even heard of, but it sounded delicious, and he wished he could have had the chance to taste some of it, just once.

With July came even wetter weather as the glacier looming above them began to melt, dripping water on them until the shelter floor was flooded and had to be cleared out as the stench of dirt, rotting blubber, and stagnant water became unbearable. Bummer was helped out of the shelter by Sally and Judge, and he gulped down the fresh air as he watched the pups play on the shore. Then he looked out to sea, praying that Samson would return soon.

August 1916

After the boss's four-week deadline passed painfully by and there was still no sign of rescue, the men began making excuses as to why Shackleton hadn't yet returned. *Maybe they took a different route? Maybe they were intercepted by another ship and taken elsewhere? Maybe they stopped somewhere on the way?* Even Bummer knew that this last one was ridiculous. They all knew that there was no land between Elephant Island and South Georgia, so if Shackleton and the rest had stopped, the only place they could possibly be was at the bottom of the Weddell Sea. The one thing that none of them dared to say out loud was this: *What if they are never coming back?*

Bummer tried to be as optimistic as Samson, telling himself that it could be any day now. Any day, they would look out and see a boat on the horizon coming to save them all. But for Bummer, with the infection raging through his body, it already felt too late.

Sally came to sit beside him as they watched the men arguing for the fifth time that day about what they should do next. After Shackleton had left, Wild had instructed the men each day to gather everything together so they'd be ready when the boat came to pick them up, telling them, "The boss could arrive today!"

But as the days drew on, they eventually gave up, deciding not to waste precious energy on something that was likely to be fruitless. Wild yelled at the men that they would have to go out on the boats themselves, and some of the other men shut up at this, not wanting to take the risk, especially as the boats were hardly fit for such a journey since they had been turned into living quarters, and the men no longer had the carpenter around to make the boats seaworthy.

"How are you feeling?" Sally asked Bummer gently as he smiled to himself. He'd been thinking of something but couldn't quite remember what.

"I'm feeling fine, Sally," he croaked. "Don't you worry about me."

Sally looked back at Judge hovering nearby and shook her head slightly.

"Well, you just hold on for a while longer," Sally told him. "Samson will be back soon. I am sure of it."

"Samson," Bummer repeated, suddenly remembering.

He had been thinking about Samson and the day they had met. Samson had stood up for Bummer when no other dog would.

"Samson," he mumbled, immediately forgetting the thought again.

He let his eyes drift slowly shut as the sounds of the men arguing and Sally talking in a low voice beside him faded. His final thought was that he wished he could have seen his friend Samson one last time.

CHAPTER 26
SALLY

August 30, 1916

Sally watched with a sense of pride as her pups worked away with the men down on the shore. That morning, the sky had cleared, and the weather was calmer than it had been for months.

Nell barked, and one of the men went over to her, bending to dislodge a limpet she had found clinging beneath a rock. They often went down at low tide to find limpets, crabs, or anything else they could add to their dwindling rations. Sally didn't much like the salty taste or the squelchy, slimy feel of them as they slipped down her throat, but the food kept her strong for another day, and that was all she really cared about.

She gazed out to sea, able to see much farther than usual as the fog of the past few days had all but disappeared. She thought she caught something dark on the horizon and moved closer to shore, squinting as she tried to make out what she had spotted. It could be a whale, she thought. They sometimes came closer to the bay on clearer days, when there was less chance of their being accidentally beached. But they usually visited in late afternoon or as the sun was setting.

Sally continued to track the dark spot, unsure whether to get the men's attention. Whatever it was, it was definitely moving closer. It had gone from a small black speck to a bigger blot. As it moved toward the bay, Sally could make out its outline. It sailed on top of the water, not within it as a whale or seal might, and as it turned slightly to the left, Sally knew for certain what she was looking at, although she could hardly believe her eyes.

"A boat!" she barked, running to the water's edge. "I see a boat!"

The men shouted back up to camp and hurried to make a fire, gathering together blubber and paraffin. In their haste, they used too much paraffin, and as they dropped the lit match onto it, it exploded with a great *whoosh* of fire and smoke. Then, as quickly as it had ignited, it went out again, with only a few stubborn flames continuing to burn on the ground.

It didn't matter, as the ship had already seen them. It hoisted its flag, and the men gave a loud cheer, waving at their rescuers. When the ship could come no farther because of the risk of running against the rocks, it lowered its anchor, then let down a small boat over the side. Sally could just make out three figures in the boat, two men waving back at them and one large dog, wagging his tail back and forth.

"Samson!" Sally whispered as tears filled her eyes.

"Samson!" her pups cried, running to tell the other dogs. "It's Samson!"

Samson

They had made numerous attempts to find their way back to Elephant Island, but each mission had been thwarted by bad weather or hindered by pack ice or some other obstacle that had forced them to turn back.

The longer time went on, the more frustrated Samson felt. They had promised to return after four weeks. What must Bummer and Sally be thinking? That they had been abandoned?

Samson hoped his friends knew that he would never give up, but what could he do? He was just a dog. He couldn't commandeer a ship or sail to his friends' rescue. The boss had exhausted almost every avenue possible. There were few ships that could make the crossing to Elephant Island and even fewer captains willing to try. Just when all seemed lost, the Chilean government offered the boss the use of one of its ships—the *Yelcho*. But Samson knew this was their last chance. He'd overheard the boss saying that if they didn't make it this time, the British government would take over the rescue mission and it would be out of their hands. Samson might never have the chance to go back or see his friends again.

As the imposing outline of Elephant Island finally appeared on the horizon, Samson felt his stomach lurch with emotion—he couldn't tell if he was more excited, nervous, or afraid of what they might find. Would anyone be there to greet them when they arrived?

His fears were short-lived. As they came in view of the bay, Samson could already see some of the men and dogs hailing them. Shackleton and Crean rushed to the *Yelcho*'s small lifeboat, and Samson bounded across the deck, determined not to be left behind. He leaped into the boat before either man had time to protest. The boat was slowly lowered to the water, and a flash of fear sparked in Samson's stomach as he remembered the journey in the *James Caird* and how close they had come so many times to not making it back to Elephant Island at all.

As Crean rowed them to shore, Shackleton took out his binoculars to get a better view of his men. Samson could hear him quietly counting the men under his breath, and Samson began doing the same with the dogs. He quickly spotted Wolf and Hercules, as they were still great lumbering beasts despite having lost weight. Judge was off to one side, his back turned as though he was looking back up to their camp. But there was no sign of Sally and the pups. Or Bummer.

"Are you all well?" Shackleton called out as they neared shore.

"All well, boss!" the men replied as they assembled

in a line on the beach to greet him. Not one man was missing. Twenty-two men, all present and accounted for. Against all odds, they had made it.

Samson scanned the beach again desperately, hoping that the same could be said for the dogs. Suddenly, from behind the lifeboats, which had been stacked one on top of the other, Sally emerged, shortly followed by one, two, three . . . four puppies! Samson allowed himself to breathe again, until he realized there was still no sign of Bummer.

The men ran to meet the boat, dragging it up onto the shore as they greeted their boss. Samson leaped into the water, weaving his way between their legs and sniffing the ground for the scent of his best friend. Judge came over to greet him with a shake of his tail.

"You are a sight for sore eyes," Judge said.

Samson smiled. "It's good to see you again, Judge."

He looked up as the puppies, now fully grown dogs, bounded toward him, asking so many questions at once that he couldn't understand a word any of them was saying.

"Give him room to breathe," Sally told them. "You'll have plenty of time to catch up on the journey home."

She looked up at Samson and smiled, her eyes sparkling.

"Bummer?" Samson whispered.

Sally lowered her eyes and had opened her mouth to speak when a movement behind Samson caught his eye. He turned to look back at the camp. Bummer was slowly making his way toward him, limping as he held up his front leg, heavily wrapped in a bandage. Samson raced over to his friend, almost knocking him over as he skidded to a stop.

"Bummer!" Samson cried. "I thought...when I didn't see you on the beach, I thought I might have lost you."

Bummer beamed back at his friend. "Well, you almost did," he admitted.

That was when Samson noticed that not only was Bummer thinner than all the other dogs, his fur duller, but his front leg also ended in a stump where his paw should have been.

"What happened?" Samson whispered.

"Leopard seal," Bummer replied. "I was almost on my way out when Dr. Macklin decided to take drastic action and chopped off my paw." He gave a small smile. "Of course, it would have been polite if he'd consulted me first, but I wasn't really in any fit state to protest, and besides," he said, lifting his leg slightly, "I'd lose my paw again in a heartbeat if it meant being here for this moment."

Samson walked slowly beside his friend as he hobbled down to the shore, where the men were already loading the boat with supplies and anything else they wanted to take with them.

An hour later, they were all safely on board the *Yelcho*, heading back to South Georgia and whatever lay ahead.

"So," Bummer asked, "did you get the adventure you were looking for?"

Samson considered this for a while, watching the men and surviving dogs as they hugged and barked and cried.

"I've seen and done things I never thought possible," he said finally. "We've journeyed to places where no other dog in the world has ever set a paw before."

He nudged his friend's shoulder with his head. "How about you, Bummer?"

Bummer thought for a moment. "I found a place I belong," he said.

Samson raised an eyebrow.

"Not the Antarctic, obviously," Bummer added with a grin. "I think my days of exploration are over. But you and Sally and the pups...even Wolf and Hercules feel more like family to me than my own ever did."

"Do you know the most amazing thing of all?" Samson asked. He lifted his nose toward the men. All twenty-eight of them still in one piece...more or less. "They survived," he continued. "Every single man on this expedition. Against all odds, and everything that was thrown at us."

He leaned his head gently against Bummer's and whispered, "We survived."

Author's Note

The story of Shackleton's *Endurance* expedition is such an amazing tale of survival because despite incredible odds—and due in no small part to the absolute determination of Shackleton to get his crew home safely—every single man on the expedition survived. This means that there are many books, diaries, and other accounts by the men themselves, including Shackleton's documentation of the extraordinary expedition.

Frank Hurley, the photographer, was also able to save many of his photographs and much of his film, which he sealed in watertight metal tins. As the wreck of the *Endurance* began sinking, he and Shackleton dived beneath the icy water to retrieve as much as they could.

Thanks to their bravery and foresight, we can still see the haunting images of the *Endurance* today.

While I have taken some creative license with parts of the story, many of the things that happened to Bummer and Samson in the book did actually happen on the expedition—but to the men.

The seal attack, for example, when the men were running desperately low on food and provisions, occurred on a day when a seal jumped out at one of the crew (Thomas Orde-Lees). Luckily, Frank Wild was on hand to shoot the seal, and they did in fact find that it had a belly full of fish, saving the starving men.

Mrs. Chippy also started off the adventure with a quick dip in the ocean and was saved by one of the crew. Holness did, in fact, fall into the water when the ice floe split beneath the men's tents, but it was Shackleton himself who saved the man, and not one of the dogs.

Sadly, unlike in this book, none of the dogs made it safely home. When the men sailed to Elephant Island, the dogs were deemed more of a burden than a help, and the adventure continued without them.

ENDURANCE
IN ANTARCTICA

FACT FILE

Animals on the Imperial Trans-Antarctic Expedition

- During the expedition, the crew spotted many different types of wildlife, including whales, penguins, seals, and seabirds.

- Ninety-nine dogs were sent from Canada to Shackleton in London, to be used to pull the sleds and equipment across Antarctica. On Shackleton's previous expedition to Antarctica, he had used ponies, but he'd found that they were unsuited for the harsh conditions, so he followed explorer Roald Amundsen's example and decided to take dogs.

- Of those ninety-nine dogs, sixty-five were chosen for the expedition. They were specifically selected for their size, strength, and ability to withstand the freezing temperatures of the Antarctic. They were all very large dogs—mixtures of Newfoundlands, Saint Bernards, wolfhounds, wolves, and Eskimo dogs—and weighed around a hundred pounds each.

- The dogs were named by Shackleton and the crew during the crossing over the Weddell Sea. Each man was allocated a group of dogs to look after.

- The dogs' names were:

Alti	Brownie	Elliott
Amundsen	Buller	Fluff
Blackie	Bummer	Gruss
Bob	Caruso	Hackenschmidt
Bo'sun	Chips	Hercules
Bristol	Dismal	Jamie

Jasper	Roy	Side Lights
Jerry	Rufus	Simian
Judge	Rugby	Slippery Neck
Luke	Sadie	Slobbers
Lupoid	Sailor	Snowball
Mack	Saint	Soldier
Martin	Sally	Songster
Mercury	Sammy	Sooty
Noel	Samson	Spider
Paddy	Sandy	Split Lip
Peter	Satan	Spotty
Rodger	Shakespeare	Steamer

Steward	Surly	Upton
Stumps	Swanker	Wallaby
Sub	Sweep	Wolf
Sue	Tim	

- Sally's puppies: Nell, Nelson, Roger, and Toby

- As well as dogs, there was also a ship's cat called Mrs. Chippy, who belonged to the carpenter, McNish. McNish brought his beloved cat along with him, and although she was called Mrs. Chippy, it turned out that she was male.

Animal Facts

SLED DOGS

- Like Shackleton's dogs, sled dogs are chosen for their size, strength, speed, thick fur, and ability to run long distances.

- They can race across the ice as fast as twenty miles per hour.

- Alaska hosts an annual sled race called the Iditarod, where people known as mushers race with teams of sixteen dogs over a thousand miles.

- Each dog team has a leader.

- Each dog has a separate harness that is attached to a main line leading to the sled.

- Dogs have been used to pull sleds for thousands of years. As modern modes of transportation were invented, sled dogs came to be used only for racing.

LEOPARD SEALS

- Leopard seals often ambush their prey beneath the water or by leaping out of the sea onto ice shelves. With long, sharp teeth and powerful jaws, they eat fish, penguins, birds, and the young pups of smaller types of seals.

- Female leopard seals are larger than males. They can grow to be ten feet long and can weigh up to a thousand pounds.

- As with whales and penguins, the thick layer of blubber beneath their skin keeps them warm in the freezing temperatures of the Antarctic.

- They are the second-largest species of seal in the world and are one of Antarctica's most dangerous predators, second only to the killer whale.

- The leopard seal became known as the leopard of the sea because of the spotted pattern of its skin.

WHALES

- Many species of whale are found in the Antarctic, including killer whales, blue whales, humpback whales, and sperm whales.

- Killer whales, also known as orcas, hunt in groups known as pods for penguins, seals, sharks, and smaller whales.

- Whales can be found in every ocean on Earth. Killer whales' rows of sharp teeth and ability to hunt in groups make them the deadliest predator in the Antarctic.

- The blue whale is the largest creature on the planet, measuring over 100 feet long and weighing up to 170 tons.

- The sperm whale can dive down to seven thousand feet and can remain underwater for an hour and a half.

Expedition Facts

- Five thousand men applied to go on the expedition, but only twenty-six were chosen. Blackborow, the stowaway, joined the expedition in Buenos Aires.

- The crew were:

  - Frank Worsley—ship's captain

  - Ernest Shackleton—expedition leader

  - Frank Wild—second-in-command

  - Leonard Hussey—meteorologist

- George Marston—artist

- Walter How—able seaman

- Reginald James—physicist

- Thomas Orde-Lees—motor expert and store keeper

- John Vincent—boatswain and able seaman

- Tom Crean—second officer

- William Stephenson—fireman and stoker

- Robert Clark—biologist

- James Wordie—geologist

- Timothy McCarthy—able seaman

- Alfred Cheetham—third officer

- Frank Hurley—photographer

- Dr. James McIlroy—second surgeon

- Dr. Alexander Macklin—surgeon

- Lionel Greenstreet—first officer

- Ernest Holness—able seaman and stoker

- Huberht Hudson—navigating officer

- Charles Green—cook

- Alexander Kerr—second engineer

- Louis Rickinson—chief engineer

- Thomas McLeod—able seaman

- Henry McNish—ship's carpenter

- William Bakewell—able seaman

- Perce Blackborow—stowaway

- The *Endurance* got its name from Ernest Shackleton's family motto: "By endurance, we conquer."

- Shackleton had previously been on two other expeditions to Antarctica: the *Discovery* expedition with the famous explorer Captain Robert Falcon Scott, and the *Nimrod* expedition. On the first expedition, Shackleton became ill and had to return home. On the second expedition, the group took along ponies rather than dogs and were forced to turn around after running out of food.

- Along with the photographer, Hurley, there was also an artist on board called George Marston, who captured the expedition through his paintings. When left behind on Elephant Island, he was the one who had the idea to make shelters out of the lifeboats and use his oil paints as glue.

- The *Endurance* crew were away from home for almost two years and spent 497 days on the water or ice floes.

- Shackleton and his crew were only one part of the expedition. Another group called the Ross party was sent from New Zealand to the opposite side of Antarctica, with the goal of setting up supply depots for Shackleton's party, as they were not able to carry enough provisions to take them the whole way across Antarctica. Unfortunately, the ice pulled the Ross party's ship, the *Aurora,* away from some of the sledding parties on the ice, leaving those men marooned as the damaged ship was forced to return to New Zealand. The Ross sea party remained stranded until the *Aurora* was fixed and returned to rescue them in January 1917.

Timeline

1914

August 1: The *Endurance* departs London on the same day that Germany declares war on Russia, signaling the start of World War I.

August 4: Britain declares war on Germany. Shackleton offers his ship and crew to the British government for the war effort.

August 8: Shackleton receives a one-word telegram from the Admiralty—*Proceed*. The *Endurance* departs from Plymouth.

October 26: With the final crew on board, the *Endurance* leaves Buenos Aires, Argentina, for South Georgia, an island in the South Atlantic. The crew spends a month making final preparations at Grytviken whaling station.

December 5: The *Endurance* departs Grytviken, heading for the South Sandwich Islands.

December 7: They encounter pack ice and have to carefully navigate the shifting passages of water.

1915

January 10: The first sighting of Antarctica. Progress through the narrow leads of pack ice is very slow.

January 18: Ice closes in around the ship and it becomes stuck. They wait for the ice to shift for ten days, putting out the ship's fires to conserve fuel.

February 14: They try to break free of the ice. For over forty-eight hours, the crew attacks the ice with chisels, picks, and saws. The ship moves a little way before becoming stuck once more. They are only one day's sail from land.

February 22: The ice begins to drift north, taking the *Endurance* with it—and farther away from Antarctica.

February 24: The *Endurance* becomes the crew's winter base. The crew trains the dogs and prepares for when the ice breaks up. A dog town is built and "dogloos" are made from wood and snow. The inside of the ship is remodeled, and the ship becomes known as the Ritz, after the famous hotel.

May 1: The sun vanishes, not to be seen again for four months. The landscape becomes more difficult to navigate as pressure ridges rise up and threaten to crush the ship.

June 22: The crew celebrates Midwinter's Day with a feast, speeches, songs, toasts, and a rousing rendition of the British national anthem. The crew holds an Antarctic Derby, with Frank Wild snatching an exciting victory over Frank Hurley.

July: Blizzards make a mess of the ship. In early July the sun begins to return, but the ice continues to buckle. For safety, the men and dogs evacuate the ice and new kennels are built on the upper deck.

August 1: The ship lists heavily to port.

September 1: Ice begins to break up the ship. Shackleton and Wild inspect the damage, and the crew cuts the ice away as best they can.

September 2: Pressure ice makes the *Endurance* jump into the air and settle on its beam.

October 27: Ice opens planks in the hull on the starboard side, letting water in. The crew works the pumps for three days and nights. At five PM Shackleton gives the order to abandon ship. Stores and equipment are taken off the ship to set up camp, and sleds are packed with as many supplies as possible. The reduced provisions are put into three of the four lifeboats.

November 1: The nearest land is 350 miles west. The men march, pulling the lifeboats. After three days, they are still in sight of the ship. They erect Ocean Camp, which becomes their home for the next two months. Each morning, teams set out under Frank Wild's supervision to salvage boats, sledges, rations, fuel, and equipment from the wreckage of the *Endurance*.

November 21: Five PM. With a cry of "She's going, boys!" Shackleton and the crew watch the *Endurance* sink into the Weddell Sea. The drift has carried them thirteen hundred miles.

December 22: All luxury food for Christmas is eaten up, including mince pies, Christmas pudding, tea and cocoa, baked beans, and anchovies in oil.

December 23: They begin to march again toward open water, averaging a mile and a half a day, pulling heavily loaded sledges and boats for seven days and seven nights.

December 29: Shackleton abandons the march to set up Patience Camp, where they stay for three and a half months. Hunting becomes the crew's main activity. Sled teams are sent out in search of seals and penguins as rations run low.

1916

January 21: A blizzard blows the camp south toward the Antarctic Circle.

February 29: In honor of leap-year day, the crew enjoys three full meals. The crew spends time hunting, reading, repairing and drying their clothes, making weather observations, and taking scientific measurements. Hurley creates a stove fueled by blubber.

March 30: With warmer weather approaching, the ice begins to weaken. This was the end of the journey for the dogs.

March 31: The ice begins to disintegrate. The floe they are on splits in two, separating them from the lifeboats, but they manage to get the boats back. They make plans to head out on the lifeboats.

April 7: Elephant Island appears on the horizon.

April 9: After six months, they head out onto water in the three lifeboats: the *James Caird*, the *Dudley Docker*, and the *Stancomb Wills*. It is so cold that the men's hands have to be chipped away from the oars and their joints seize up. They each eat only one biscuit—a plain cookie—a day.

April 16: After seven grueling days at sea, the lifeboats land safely on Elephant Island. The crew kills seals, eating and drinking their first hot meal in days.

April 17: The island has no shelter from the wind, cold, and rain. Shackleton moves camp seven miles to the west and calls it Wild Camp. The lifeboats land in sleet and gales, so the men shelter beneath the boats. The blizzard rages for five days.

April 20: Shackleton announces that he will attempt to sail the twenty-two-and-a-half-foot *James Caird* 800 miles to South Georgia. McNish, the carpenter, sets to work—fitting canvas over the top of the boat and loading it with ballast, along with water-filled kegs and food to last four weeks.

April 22: McNish finishes work and the weather clears.

April 24: Shackleton, Tom Crean, Frank Worsley, Timothy McCarthy, Henry McNish, and John Vincent set off for South Georgia across the world's most dangerous ocean. Frank Wild is left in charge of the men on Elephant Island, where bad weather settles in. Marston, the artist, has the idea to make the boats into a shelter.

They turn the boats upside down and use his oil paints as glue to secure canvas sheets over the hulls for extra protection. They insert chimneys through the hulls, raise the boats off the ground, and carve a gutter around the outside to avoid getting wet. Wild gives the men jobs to keep them busy, and at night Hussey plays his banjo.

On the *Caird*, the weather is severe. The men work in four-hour shifts. Three sleep below the canvas among the ballast while three remain above. Worsley navigates by using the sun's position and his own intuition.

May 7: On the fourteenth day at sea, they spot signs that land is near—birds in the sky and seaweed in the water.

May 10: After seventeen days, the *James Caird* miraculously arrives on the west coast of South Georgia. They sail into King Haakon Bay but realize that the whaling station is on the opposite side of the island. They will have to go over the island on foot, over peaks and glaciers never crossed before.

May 19: Shackleton, Worsley, and Crean set off to cross the glacier-clad peaks. They screw nails into their boots for extra grip and set off, leaving the ill men behind. With an ax and a rope as their only equipment, they set out at three AM by the light of a full moon.

May 20: At 6:30 AM, after trekking without a break for thirty-six hours, the men arrive at Stromness whaling station.

May 23: The men depart on the English-owned *Southern Sky* to rescue the men on Elephant Island but are stopped by ice a hundred miles short of the island. The men left behind on the other side of South Georgia are rescued and given passage home.

June 10: The Uruguayan government loans the survey ship *Instituto de Pesca No 1.* The ship comes in sight of Elephant Island before pack ice forces the crew to turn back.

July 12: Chartered by the British Association, the schooner *Emma* sets out from Punta Arenas, Chile, again traveling a hundred miles short of Elephant Island before storms and ice force it to return.

August 25: Chilean authorities loan the *Yelcho*, a small steamer, which sets sail with Shackleton, Worsley, and Crean for Elephant Island on their fourth attempt.

August 30: Eighteen weeks after Shackleton set out from Elephant Island, he returns on the *Yelcho*, rescuing all crew members.

September 3: The *Yelcho* reaches Punta Arenas with all twenty-eight men of the *Endurance* expedition.

Glossary

ADMIRALTY: the government department that ran the British navy

BALLAST: heavy material carried by a boat or ship to add weight for extra stability

BLUBBER: the fat layer of a whale or seal, found between skin and muscle; can be used as fuel

BOW: the front of a ship

CREVICE: a crack, as in ice, that forms an opening

FISSURE: a narrow opening

FLANK: to stand at the side of someone or something

FLOE: a sheet of floating ice on the surface of the sea

FOOTBALL: the British word for soccer

FUNNEL: the smokestack of a steamship

GALLEY: the kitchen on a ship

GANGPLANK: a flat plank that leads from a ship to the dock or ground

GEE: a command meaning "right"

GLACIER: an extended mass of slowly moving ice built up over many years

HAW: a command meaning "left"

HOOSH: a thick stew made from dried meat, fat, cereal, biscuits, and water

HULL: the hollow, lowermost part of a ship

JIB BOOM: a strong, thick pole extending from the bow of a ship, used to secure the headsail

LEAD: a passage of water through an ice floe

MUSH: a command meaning "go"

PACK: a group of dogs

PEMMICAN: a mixture of dried meat and fat

PENINSULA: an area of land almost completely surrounded by water apart from a single point connecting it to a mainland

POD: a group of whales

PORT: the left-hand side of a ship

PRECIPICE: a cliff with a steep vertical drop

PROVISIONS: supplies of food and other necessities

QUAYSIDE: the edge of a dock where it meets water

RUNT: the smallest or weakest animal in a litter

STARBOARD: the right-hand side of a ship

STEAMER: a ship run by coal and steam

STERN: the back end of a ship

STOWAWAY: a person who hides aboard a ship without permission

TELEGRAM: a message or communication

WHEELHOUSE: the part of the ship that houses the ship's wheel

WHOA: a command meaning "stop"

WILDERNESS: a wild, uninhabited area

Further Reading

BOOKS

Alexander, Caroline. *The Endurance*. New York: Knopf, 1998. (Features many of the amazing photographs Frank Hurley took on the expedition.)

Armstrong, Jennifer. *Shipwreck at the Bottom of the World*. New York: Knopf Books for Young Readers, 2000.

Bertozzi, Nick. *Shackleton: Antarctic Odyssey*. New York: First Second, 2014.

Buckley, James. *Who Was Ernest Shackleton?* New York: Penguin Workshop, 2013.

Grill, William. *Shackleton's Journey*. London: Flying Eye Books, 2014.

McCurdy, Michael. *Trapped by the Ice!* New York: Walker and Co., 1997. Reprint, Bloomsbury USA Children's, 2002.

Shackleton, Ernest. *South: The Illustrated Story of Shackleton's Last Expedition.* Minneapolis: Zenith Press, 2016.

WEBSITES

bbc.co.uk/history/historic_figures/shackleton_ ernest.shtml

ernestshackleton.net

jamescairdsociety.com

shackletonfoundation.org

shackleton100.com

DOCUMENTARY

NOVA: *Shackleton's Voyage of Endurance*, aired March 26, 2002, on PBS, http://www.pbs.org/wgbh/nova/ shackleton.

Scott Palmieri

Katrina Charman lives in a small village in the middle of Southeast England with her husband and three daughters. Katrina has wanted to be a children's writer ever since she was eleven, when her schoolteacher set her class the task of writing an epilogue to Roald Dahl's *Matilda*. Her teacher thought her writing was good enough to send to Roald Dahl himself. Sadly, she never got a reply, but the experience ignited her love of reading and writing. She invites you to visit her online at katrinacharman.com.

EM*BARK* ON INCREDIBLE HISTORICAL ADVENTURES

WITH

SURVIVAL TAILS!